with love new
reader,

James Dent .

x

HERON
AND
ASAPH

The emergence of the Divine Feminine.
A story for our time.

JANICE DENT

T

The manufacturer's authorised representative in the EU for product safety is Authorised Rep Compliance Ltd, 71 Lower Baggot Street, Dublin D02 P593 Ireland (www.arccompliance.com)

Troubador Publishing Ltd
Unit E2 Airfield Business Park,
Harrison Road, Market Harborough,
Leicestershire. LE16 7UL
Tel: 0116 2792299
Email: books@troubador.co.uk
Web: www.troubador.co.uk

ISBN 978 1836282 884

British Library Cataloguing in Publication Data.
A catalogue record for this book is available from the British Library.

Printed and bound in Great Britain by 4edge Limited
Typeset in 11pt Minion Pro by Troubador Publishing Ltd, Leicester, UK

For Ruby, Edward and Grace

Foreword

The very nature of life is change; it may be hard to embrace, but this is an eternal truth. Our planet, Mother Earth, is our life, and she is changing. This is happening now. We are part of her, we are of her body, we are nature. So, we, too, are changing with her.

Within each person, regardless of gender, lies an interweaving of masculine and feminine energies. Our masculine nature deals with our relationship to the outer world. It is assertive, intellectual, authoritative; it gets things done. Our feminine principle is concerned with our inner world. Gentle and nurturing, receptive, creative and compassionate; it is where our intuition lies.

It is the masculine aspect that we favour and, indeed, worship in our societies. We are out of balance.

Mother Earth brings herself back into balance within the ever-changing universe, and she brings us back into balance, too. That we may create our lives from a place of inner harmony. There is a wave, a rising tide. There is a buoying of the feminine energies at this time, that they may balance with the dominant masculine aspect and be integrated into the whole. Balance, balance, always balance.

This is a story of the expression of this phenomenon of

change, as it unfolded within me on my journey towards balance and wholeness. It began in another time and place. I found Heron in my visions, a representation of the wound of my sacred feminine aspect and its potential to heal. And through the Law of Attraction, I found Asaph – an expression of my own sacred masculine nature. It is a story, a fable, for everyone at this time of change and rebalancing. Listen for the feminine calling within you. Welcome her back.

Part One

HERON

1

Heron was ten years old. She did not speak; she had never spoken. More went in than out. She was absorbent.

The marketplace was alive and thronging. It was familiar to her, exciting, alarming almost; an invigorating assault on her senses. Hot sand burned beneath her feet; hot people buffeted her in flapping robes; there were no heads that she could see. Her view was only of tunics and feet churning up clouds of dust as her mother dragged her through the crowds. She squinted her eyes against the billowing dirt and blinked away its gritty intrusion. Her small shoulders were raised and braced as if they might protect her senses from the onslaught. Her mother's grip on her wrist was unyielding and comforting in equal measure. Tight but safe from being swept away.

As she was pulled along, Heron's attention was captivated by two tall, black bulbous jars. She craned her neck and blinked her watery eyes; she had never seen any so big – almost as big as the young boy who was dragging them off the cart. They had been strapped on with leather bindings in some artful arrangement of interlocking knots and lacing, which the boy seemed to know the magic code of unravelling. Something about this impressed her. He skilfully unloaded, rolled and shuffled the giant jars over to a market stall. The merchant was unimpressed. He didn't acknowledge the boy's effort, his expertise, his dedication, his endeavour. He was met with ignorance and contempt.

Heron watched the small drama unfold. The hardness of the energy between the man and the boy. The deflation of the boy, the stab of his hurt, the erosion of his worthiness, his stifled resentment, the rising anger in them both. The man flicked a coin, which bounced in the dust. His intention was to make the boy forage in the dirt to retrieve it. He sealed his loathing and made sure the boy knew his value was unrecognised. He had taken a small piece of the boy's dignity along with the oil he had delivered.

In the three or four paces it had taken to pass by, Heron had felt the pain of them both. The pain of having a tender heart and the pain of having a hard heart. This was her gift. She felt everything. But it was also a burden that weighed heavily upon her. It was hard to be sensitive in an insensitive world.

The chaos of the market had thrust her back into the real world. She spent most of her time slightly elevated from it, being moved by finer currents. In a flow that runs through life unseen, but with an intelligence of its own. This was the space she mostly inhabited.

2

Heron was quietly revered by her mother for this unnamed trait. She wasn't chastised or ridiculed. Her mother seemed to understand intuitively that this was her uniqueness. Her detachment was the source, or maybe the product of some mysterious gift. She did not understand it; her child was, in many ways, unfathomable to her. But what she knew with crystal clarity, born of her finely tuned motherly instinct, was that her complete acceptance was the greatest gift she could give to Heron. To allow her to be as she was. There was a deep knowing in her that not only was this strangeness allowable, but it was, in some way, a precious attribute. She possessed a purity, somehow untouched by the murkiness of life.

And so, she felt protective of this innocence in her child. But at the same time, Heron's innocence seemed to give the child a clear and unfettered wisdom, which somehow made her feel as though it was *she* who was the child, not Heron.

The woman pondered this curious paradox as she ran her eyes and hands absently over bales of finely woven fabric. She wistfully watched her mysterious daughter appraising the marketplace from a vantage point she knew was different from her own. Her stillness, her view of the market and, indeed, of life somehow not limited by her bodily senses. It was as if she possessed an extra sense, a perspective that appeared to endow her with some unspoken wisdom. Some knowing. The mother loved her, but sensed that the thread connecting their hearts was very long. Heron was her own free entity and part of Heron did not seem to be attached to her in the usual way a child clings to its mother. It was as if she had some other alternative security.

She stroked the soft cloth and watched her daughter standing there. Her body was there in the marketplace, her thin brown arms and legs as real as any other child's, and yet some other part of her was expanded somehow to encompass more than she could comprehend. But it was fine. Her love for Heron allowed that she wasn't completely here and she accepted her own faint knowing that she may have to let Heron go one day to where this mystery was in her.

She smiled gently. Her heart yielded with softness as she watched her child watching life. And she stroked the fabric softly. She contemplated how Heron did not speak. It was as if words were too jarring, too clumsy and bulky for the finer vibrations that she inhabited. But a tender love was woven between them, like the soft threads beneath her hands. It was all that was required of her as a mother, it seemed, to nurture the soft threads that bound them.

The woman was startled from her reverie.

"Are you buying?!" The stallholder banged his fist down on the bale inches from her own. She recoiled in alarm, her nerves jangled by his brutishness, his ugliness, his rank breath as he jutted his face towards her. Shaken, she recoiled and, without speaking, she stepped away. Was this the same harsh assault that Heron felt all the time, with most of life? She suspected it was. For a moment, she understood her daughter's preference for staying in the safety of her detached observation. She stroked Heron's hair and the threads between them relaxed into a resonance of understanding. Their tapestry.

3

Together, mother and daughter returned to their home. Heron sat outside alone, cross-legged on the earth, shaded by the wall at the side of their dwelling. This was her favourite spot, out of the afternoon sun and also out of the view of life passing by behind her. She picked the tiny particles of dust from her hair.

Her fingers pulled slowly and methodically through her dark hair, tangled with the dust of the market. As she smoothed out the strands, it soothed her, and with it she smoothed out the discordant energy of the exchange with the boy and the oil seller that she had absorbed. She let the harshness flow away as her fingers returned both her hair and her nerves to an equilibrium. How did her fingers do that?

She put her hands out in front of her, her gaze exploring their meaning. She examined every line of their form in great detail. The delicate crescent moons on the ends of her nails, as white and pure as moonlight. The lumpy knuckles reminded her of the crude but functional joints of the oil merchant's cart she had seen in the market. She turned them over, pondering, knowing somehow that hands were more than just claws to dig into bread, or fists to bang onto fabric bales.

She sat in the stillness with her back to the passageway down the side of the house, the passage an interface with this earthly life on the street beyond. And she sank back into the sanctuary that was her detachment from it. She slid into the feelings of the firmament, some inner vision divining its way among the stars and the galaxies. It was the moon that anchored her to Earth, in this galaxy in which everything spun and moved in perfect harmony. She felt safe in the rules. The unbreakable certainty of the rules of the firmament. It made her relax. It was home. Some part of her was as enormous as the universe. It gave her comfort. This was where she belonged. This was where she was from and where she would return. It was completely clear to her that her descent into this hostile dysregulated world in which she found herself was merely a brief phase of encasement in this human body. She accepted this as the way of things.

What she knew – the hidden realms – seemed such a precious and fragile truth, which would be destroyed by the violence of the people if they knew. So, she kept her silence. Her mouth wouldn't seem to open. The images remained inside, unshared, safe, protected. It was all too fine and beautiful, a harmonic grid of being, so far removed from this corporeal state she found herself in. Her throat constricted at the thought of confiding even to her beloved mother. It was a comfort that she seemed to respect her muteness. And her heart softened at the thought of her mother. They had a tacit understanding in which they both felt safe.

The sun had gone right down and the air was cool on her skin. She stood up, hair smoothed, nerves smoothed, and she stepped through the stone doorway of the simple home she shared with her mother. The stone portal marking her return to the density of the material world. A threshold between the two worlds she inhabited. All was well.

4

Heron stood and watched the other children playing. Her arms relaxed by her sides, open, her features calm and with a gentle, unwavering gaze. Yet an awkwardness was contained within her template of self-possession. An awkwardness, a difficulty, a dilemma at the prospect of interacting with the children and so she just watched from a distance.

They had such energy, rolling around, so physical, pushing, shouting. She tensed slightly at the impact on her delicate senses. She could go no closer.

Two boys were wrestling. Part fun, part nature, part competition. She watched them rolling in the dust. Other children came, an audience drawn to watch. They shouted encouragement, laughed and cheered and jostled as the wrestling escalated into a more wilful fight. It was a mystery to her, this behaviour.

There was a victor. A boy declared himself the champion, sweaty, staggering, arms raised aloft as his rival lay defeated in the dust. He received the applause, the cheers and accolades and she watched his ego – a false and flimsy part of him – inflate. The part of him that was compelled to pick the fight in the first place. That weak and frightened part born from his life of being made powerless himself. The part that had been repeatedly disempowered by others now felt temporarily elated, relieved of its suffering, inflated like a balloon of stolen glory.

He had replenished his empty cup of power by taking it from his opponent, who lay depleted and crestfallen in the dirt.

The victor felt her eyes watching him and, in his emboldened hubris, something made him stride over to her, grinning with an air of defiance and pride. As he approached, Heron saw that he was the boy from the market the day before who had delivered the huge oil jars. And at once she saw the endless cycle of power-snatching. The boy had lost his dignity at the hands of the oil merchant. It hurt. So, he must hurt another to replenish the loss with another's power to make himself feel better. The dance of the tender heart and the hard heart.

He stopped before her and their energies collided. His hubris, his false power met her compassion, her authentic power, with a jolt. No words were spoken. She looked into the boy's eyes. Compassion arose naturally in her for the wounded fearful child she saw within him. He was captive in her soft gaze. Her heart held his fear. For as long as it would take, she would hold him.

Feelings welled up inside of him, waves of pain and hurt and injustice. He stayed rooted to the spot. He seemed to have no choice. As if the cloak of pride from his victory was gently removed to expose the pain beneath in her tender holding. Courageously, he stood. She had disarmed him with the tenderness of her compassion and the gentleness of her gaze. His body softened and, like her, he momentarily stood undefended.

His lips tightened as a wave of emotion crested in him and Heron's heart responded and expanded to contain his fear. A rolling tear slowly cleared a path through the dirt on his cheek, revealing fresh clean skin beneath the dust of the fight. It was done. She smiled timidly and bowed her head at his courage to stay.

All this in a matter of seconds. With confusion and some strange wonderment, he acknowledged her silently, dipping his head in the faintest bow as he returned her gaze.

He turned and walked away from the gladiator's pit that he had so proudly inhabited just moments before. He had a calmness. She had touched him in those moments more tenderly than he had ever experienced. It had ignited something in the boy. She had allowed him to feel his own true power, an inner strength all his own, accessed through his moment of vulnerability. And he took that with him. She could see it in his air and his easy gait. He had been reminded of his own source of strength that dwelt within – a rich seam of strength beside which the strength over his opponent, or the oil merchant's strength over him, felt a pale and hollow comparison.

The other children, who had been watching silently, began to disperse. Perplexed and wary, they slipped away.

Heron's mouth pursed as a wave of anxiety washed through her. What had she done?

It touched her deeply that what felt like her most sacred and private inner nature had impacted the boy. Had she touched a sacred part within him? It felt as though the magnitude of her whole cosmic being had been crystallised into a tiny droplet and fed into the boy through her eyes and it had opened up in him somehow.

She turned and walked home. She returned to her favourite place outside at the side of the house. This time, she sat with her knees tucked up close, her arms wrapped around them, balled up safe with her chin on her knees. It was as if, with the interaction with the oil seller's boy, she had been shown a doorway through which her safe inner world and this jarring outer world could intersect. A way to connect to people. She felt an overwhelming sense of awe. And with it, a weight of responsibility, a calling, a purpose. A piece of her cosmic puzzle had found its fit. This felt important, meaningful, serious.

She held her knees tightly as some formless energy reached forward and wrapped itself around her, holding her with recognition, honouring and comfort.

5

The following day, Heron sat again by the side of the house. This time, her inner vision took her down into a dark space of nothing and everything, of possibility. The brightness of the sun overhead could not illuminate this inner world of subterranean darkness she found herself in. She was in a space as vast as the cosmos, but it was empty. Black and velvety, like the primal womb of the universe. Vast, soft blackness. She placed her hands on her lower belly, a ten-year-old womb. She knew it was through her own womb she was falling, descending deep into this primordial space. She was this space.

She heard a thrumming. A heartbeat. A rhythmic pulsing of some unseen mother. Steady and relentless, she felt its vibration through the walls of the darkness. As though she was sitting in the great womb and the heartbeat was that of Mother Earth herself.

She let go and allowed the pulsing vibration to merge with her. She became the vibration. Louder and louder until her whole being was at one with the vibration of the Earth.

Heron felt safe. Another home. As though the vastness and order of the cosmic grid was an upstairs home, and this black void was a dark downstairs home.

The background rhythm of the Earth's heartbeat lulled her and she expanded into the darkness. All she could sense in the blackness was possibility. The possibility of nothing becoming something. A sense of simmering potential, a tinderbox, a scintillating mass of particles, ripe, ready. Potentiality. An atmosphere alive with these pregnant particles of possibility, shimmering, vibrating, waiting. It was as if they awaited the crack of a flint, the spark that would ignite them, the catalyst to breathe life into their potential. To provide what was necessary for their activation and the fruition of their potential. She sat in this field.

She knew that the spark that was required by the Earth resided in the cosmos, her other home. Her upstairs home. She felt the masculine nature of the cosmos; steelier, colder, unsentimental, looking for a focus, a task to complete. And yet she sat in a womb, nurturing, deep, vast, alive, simmering. Part of her was in each camp. Her head in the cosmos, her womb in the dark, pulsing void beneath, as if she spanned the divide.

She allowed herself to become one with the scintillating womb particles and they started to move. They surged up through her body, seeking, divining, reaching upwards as if magnetised by the cosmos above. Up they streamed. A Goddess burst through her head and beseeched the Gods. The cosmos responded instantaneously and the light from a distant star presented itself and served the Goddess what she desired, with a simple obedience as if it was the most natural order of things. The starlight streamed down Heron's body and into the pulsing womb space.

There was a roar; it was deafening. A sound reverberated around the void. The sound of creation. And Heron felt the deep primordial satisfaction in the Earth's body as she was served what she had asked for.

Heron sat motionless. Outwardly, she looked as though she were sitting cross-legged in the dust and sand, but inwardly she was suspended between the poles of the Earth and of the cosmos.

Her body, the vessel through which all this was happening. She waited, still and empty. A few moments passed. Then, she felt a pulsing beneath her. Her body became aware of the Earth shifting below, an energy getting closer. Her root became alive, her womb stretched with the approaching vibration, and a sudden roaring fountain of energy coursed up from the womb of the Earth, stretching her heart and bursting back out of her head, where it seemed to collide with the atmosphere and changed form. As if a fountain of hot liquid honey had left her head and met with the cold air and thickened instantly, turning into a golden gloop whose density made it fall with gravity, coating her with a thick golden covering. Something that had a quality of the energies of this earthly world, but its form was unknown to her.

The black pulsating womb space of the Earth had requested Light from the multidimensional cosmos. And from these many dimensions, it had created something; an energy, a shape, a template, an unknown thing with qualities of this earthly life that she found herself in. This earthly life that was bounded by different physical laws, it seemed. Where things had endings and beginnings, form, edges, energy contained into shapes, material things. Fewer dimensions than the cosmos from which it originated.

Heron's heart pounded. She opened her eyes and looked at the wall opposite her, a hewn rock face, a natural façade. Her eyes flickered to the right to the familiar comforting wall of the house. And she glanced left to another wall built of stone. It was too high for her to look over and it had never interested her what was beyond. It provided a boundary to her space in which she felt safe. Everything looked the same as when she had left.

She was reeling. Her heart thumped loudly in her chest and she placed a soothing hand upon it, staring at the hewn stone wall opposite. Her eyes didn't seem able to move from the spot onto which they were anchored. She stared until her body returned to her. She felt its familiarity, its belonging in this world, and she was grateful for its friendship, its housing of her. She stretched her legs out in front of her and, with bent knees, she ran her hands up and down her shins, reconnecting with her body and its place, which seemed to be anchored in the here and now of everyday reality. She felt thankful for that. She knew she needed this bodily container. She sighed deeply.

6

In the half-light of dawn, somewhere between sleep and wakefulness, Heron saw inside the Earth. It looked like networks of intersecting channels glistening with liquid metal. There were rivers of molten metal, moving, alive, pumping along, flowing through inner pathways, rivers, streams, deltas, a hidden living matrix. She saw information within the glistening flow; messages from Mother's heart. Mother's wisdom sending signals along her arteries, according to a code only she knew, out into a network of rivers and tributaries into a subterranean grid of life. Moving, changing, orchestrating, dictating the energies of the Earth. Underlying, underpinning the template she creates above.

Mother Earth is a living, breathing being. Heron felt all of this. She knew this. She knew she was Earth, that she was nature. Everything was part of Mother. In this world she now lived in, in this body, all living things were connected to this mother planet and so, too, to each other in a mesh of energy. Grids above, grids below, grids upon the earth. Everything connected and interconnected in one super-grid of it all.

It felt so clear to Heron. She could perceive all aspects of the grid and feel its power currents. The surges, the sparks, the smoothness of harmony, the jaggedness of discord. In her silent

17

world, she saw it all, she felt it all, she could encompass it all. Some fear lurked in her belly. This was so precious; instructions for the entirety of everything on Earth. She held it cupped in her hands and gently closed her hands into a ball and tucked it safely in her heart.

Her mother was calling her. Heron smiled and stirred at her voice. It was like a warm breeze blowing through her, uplifting, gently carrying her loosely swathed in the ribbons of her unconditional care. A welcomed balm for her powerful inner experience.

Her mother stood preparing food and Heron felt a sudden pull to her. She clung; her arms tight around her mother's waist, face against her soft belly, breathing a scent she had known since her first day. The feel of her was her first comfort. She felt, at that moment, that she needed her mother's body as much as she needed her own. And the soft threads between them pulsed and were nourished as comfort to them both.

And they ate together. Her mother spoke readily and shared her thoughts and the things she must do that day. These were received into Heron's silence, absorbed. They landed in her fertile inner world. She responded silently through her eyes with her heart-mind thoughts.

This was their easy arrangement. Like a familiar waveform through which they connected. Easy, harmonic, coherent. Love.

7

Heron could see camels in the distance, big hooves patting the sand. They were approaching. A man sat on a camel in front of her, still some distance away. As she watched, her heart was tight in her chest. A group of people, adults, nomads, travellers roaming the desert. They were strangers, not from here.

As she looked at the man, some strange pain asphyxiated her heart. A panic almost. She could barely breathe. It was too much for her and she turned and began to walk quickly back home. She felt the man's eyes glued onto her back, piercing her heart; they were not going to let go.

She ran into the house, dimly lit from a small window, and sat on the floor against the wall, biting her lip, body stiffening, anxious. What was this? Who was the stranger looking at her? She wanted to hide and dropped her face into her bended knees and let out some silent inner screech.

Time passed and the sun beckoned her outside to her favourite place. She knelt in the dust and sand. Her brown knees protruded from the bottom of her white tunic. She looked at them, considered them. She liked their symmetry, a comfort somehow to see her body. It kept her steady. As she relaxed, she moved her fingers in the sand, back and forth, left to right in unbroken curling patterns. The sand was so sun-baked and dry and the grains so smooth-running that it almost took on the properties of a liquid as her fingers wove rhythmic, hypnotic patterns before her eyes. It calmed her, soothed her. She kept her eyes down, and her fingers moved back and forth, back and forth.

Suddenly, her heart was gripped again in alarm – the same asphyxia as before. And she sensed a figure standing to her left. Dazzling light seemed to emanate from it, a form full of pulsating light of a frequency she could barely tolerate. She knew it was the stranger on the camel. Her eyes widened and her gaze clung to the patterns in the sand. If she ignored him, he might go away. In her peripheral vision, she could see his feet, sun browned beneath a long white robe.

He just stood. No words were exchanged but he said, "Come with me." He did not move. She nervously continued weaving her pattern in the sand as if to say she was busy. Without words, she declined. She must stay here. That was the expectation, the arrangement with her mother and she was obedient. She must stay. It was the way of things. Her gaze stayed low and the man of Light just stood, understanding.

Her heart contorted in his Light. She winced and lowered her head further as if against some shifting pain within. She exhaled and twisted and the pain passed.

"Follow me," said the man again wordlessly. Anxiety began to rise in her again, but in spite of its hold, she knew beyond doubt that she would follow this man. He was not dangerous; she didn't know what he was, but she knew that she would follow him. The agreement was silently sealed. The man started to move away. With her head still lowered, she walked a few paces behind him, out of her familiar home in some kind of hypnotic trance, magnetised, in awe. His Light obliterated everything else. It didn't matter where she was going or how long it would take, it was just happening.

She could not look up – he was too bright – but she followed his feet across open ground. She had no sense of time. He never turned; he never spoke. It was understood. She followed him into a high vaulted cave. The coolness was an instant relief from the blazing sun. Light from the entrance fell on the floor, casting rays onto which her downcast gaze was fixed. The man stopped. He sat on a rock or a ledge, she couldn't see, but he was in stillness, facing her. Her heart was now in a vice. It was hard to breathe. A terror gripped her, but not of his danger. A fear of something else worse than any danger she knew. A fear of the truth. A fear of *her* truth. A fear of exposure. Her inner world seen. Yes, a fear that this man knew all about her. She was exposed. Her safe inner world stripped bare by the Light of this man. Her defences twisted and riled against this uncovering, until they yielded and she fell to her knees before him, her eyes downcast, in surrender.

She could breathe now as she was held gently in his pulsing Light. She felt the prickling sharpness of grit pressing into her knees on the cool stony floor. Calm, and with her head bowed, she steadied herself before his feet. Their energies harmonised and her defences came away. She sighed and her body relaxed. Her mind tried to talk to her, but she couldn't hear it. It was the visceral connection between them that held her full attention. The man reached forwards with his hand and gently tilted her chin upwards. With each increment, she allowed him to raise her face; her heart tightened until she was looking in his eyes. Her heart stopped, everything stopped, she could see the whole cosmos in his eyes. Dancing turquoise light emanated from them, shimmering and illuminating his eyes with a luminous flickering dance that penetrated her own. Her heart exploded, shattered, smashed open and she wept. She was engulfed in waves of what felt like some merciful grace upon something unknown but wretched within her. Heron wept and wept and wept until no more tears came. The man waited until Heron was able to look up at him again. His energy was inviting her to do this. This time, she lifted her head by herself and gently met his eyes.

His eyes blinked slowly, conveying volumes to her. An understanding was made between them. An initiation. A wordless contract.

They left the cave side by side, her heart at peace. She held his hand. He didn't resist. He knew she would. It was right, a bond. Something fatherly, something safe. Her heart billowed with a sense of rightness, of belonging, of recognition. This man knew her in a way that her mother couldn't.

Her mother had been away collecting water. She stood by the well and looked wistfully into the distance. Absently, she ran her hand around the rim of a water jar. Slowly round and around and around as if unwinding the long thread between herself and Heron as she felt her daughter pulling away. She unwound the thread in a solemn knowing that had always resided in her heart, that one day she would lose Heron to the big mystery within her. Slowly her fingers traced the rim of the jar, loosening her bindings to her daughter. By the time her fingers stopped, she knew her daughter was gone.

She carried the water jar home, knowing that her life was changed. The water jar felt light, as if some formless being was walking with her, sharing her load. The house was empty. She did not call for Heron; she knew her daughter was gone. A pull in her heart reminded her that the thread was still attached. But she had gone. The formless being wrapped its arms around her and, in its embrace, she wept and wept and wept until no more tears came.

8

Heron walked with the man and in time they joined a group of others. No one paid her much attention and the girl sat nervously on the sand. She was in an open empty place like the desert. A woman sat down next to her and took her hand. The woman didn't go away. It was as though she was waiting for Heron to acknowledge and accept her. Heron was aware of her, but was blocking her connection. She carried on staring anxiously ahead. As the light faded, she watched a camel sit down – an ungainly collapse of its long legs until it was sitting with the others. A man was tending them. He was talking to them. He had a short stick, but he was not feeling violent. The camels were his business.

Stars began to appear in the firmament as the sky darkened. A fire crackled, the camels snorted, the camel man shuffled among them, grunting to his charges. The air was cooling and the fire was drawing the people in this group, the nomads, towards it. Several men in long robes made their way there and sat around the fire, where the man of Light was already seated. His Light, or the warmth of the fire? Which was pulling them in?

The woman holding her hand squeezed it. Heron allowed herself to acknowledge it. She looked sheepishly to her right and saw the woman was wearing dark robes. Her face was undistinguished, but it seemed to be of little consequence as her radiating kindness and a sort of eternal safety impacted Heron much more deeply than her appearance.

The woman smiled softly. She had waited patiently for Heron to acknowledge her. Her eyes were deep and swimming in some unfathomable vastness. She spoke to the girl, "I am Mariam, Mariam of Magdala." She paused and their eyes locked. "We are so glad we found you." Heron took this information in, but it didn't mean much to her. It illuminated little of her situation. Mariam squeezed her hand again. "Come," she said, starting to stand and gesturing with her eyes towards the fire. "Don't be afraid, child. I see you looking at him. His name is Yeshua. He is my husband."

Heron could not move. Mariam waited, still holding her hand. Heron just absorbed the scene. She could feel the balance, the harmony and synergy between Yeshua and Mariam. It was a field that vibrated much more intensely than with those others gathered around the fire. These were all men, a variety of different energies, but they did not have the purity, the brightness, the Light of the man Yeshua. He was like a beacon. She wondered what all this was. She felt an affinity with this woman and this man. It was as if they had the same vantage point as her own, a similar capacity. It was hard for her to define, but she knew she belonged. She stood and allowed Mariam to lead her over to the group of maybe eight or nine around the fire and she sat down. Two men were on Heron's left between her and Yeshua. Mariam sat on her right and still held her hand.

Heron was tired. The fire crackled its warm lullaby. The flames illuminated Yeshua's face as he spoke. Her head nodded and, barely realising it, she leaned into the comfort of Mariam. With her eyes closed, she could still see Yeshua and the fire. The words coming from him, his voice, his vibration, penetrated her drowsiness. Mariam lowered the sleeping girl until her head was on her lap and gently lay a blanket over her.

The woman's heart ached. She allowed herself a rare indulgence and thought of her own two daughters. Her children by Yeshua. They were far away in the care of her family, but she missed them, the physical touch of them. Her heart swelled and she sighed deeply. She looked down at Heron asleep on her lap and placed her hand on her hair. Mariam closed her eyes and a stream of locked-up, trapped mother love seemed to be released and flowed from her into this child in her lap. There was a space in Heron for it to go into. A space vacated by the absence of her own mother. It was a snug fit. Mariam sighed. She stroked the girl's hair as she slept and they were both comforted.

Mariam looked across at Yeshua. He was her equal and opposite, her reflection and she his. He was her beloved and she his. Together in this uncertain life, committed to a God that bound them. Their union was a communion with Holy Spirit. That was the centre point of them. The essence. The forms and events that unfolded in their lives from there were an outgrowth of this communion. Secondary, necessary, ordained. Events that, at this time, she sensed were uncertain, not easy and increasingly perilous.

9

When Heron woke at dawn the following day, the camp was packing up. The camels were being prepared for a journey. Heron was watching the activity through the flap of a tent. She had woken to find signs that someone had slept beside her. And she remembered Mariam. There was a crumpled mat on the ground beside hers and some belongings on the sandy floor. A small vial of oil. The other extreme to the oil jars she had seen in the market. She had never seen a jar so tiny. It intrigued her. And next to it, a string of small brown-blackish beads, long enough that it might hang around a neck, and among the small dark beads, at intervals, were larger bright green stones.

She was transfixed by these items. She would not touch them; they were not hers. But in the dawn, in the tent, in this strange new life, these items were the most impactful things in her awareness. They held her attention. They felt alive and she knew they were important. They were important to Mariam and so they seemed important to her, too.

There were voices outside the tent. Heron felt the resonance of Yeshua's voice, congruent and interweaving with Mariam's soft tones. Heron felt they were beckoning her; she was drawn to them. She rose to her feet and found herself standing outside with them in the chill of the dawn air. She didn't remember the words that were spoken, but she felt overwhelmingly special and beloved as Yeshua stood with his hand upon her shoulder. She could faintly hear their voices outside the clouds of billowing love and joy that engulfed her at being recognised and seen and acknowledged. It was an intoxication of bliss for the little girl. She didn't know why she was here, but it was glorious and her heart sang. And the billowing rapture rolled into a sense of deep devotion, of complete certainty as some thread of obedience and commitment to him sealed itself in her heart.

As she was held between them, they formed a triangle of intersecting lines, a three-way communication on many interconnecting levels, and without hearing any words she knew she would be leaving that day with Mariam. She knew Yeshua would be leaving with the men travellers and she would be leaving in another direction with Mariam, under her care, her tutelage. Heron's sense of belonging was powerful and anchoring. As if her upstairs home of the cosmos and her downstairs home of Mother Earth had come together, and with these two people, she now had her home in this material reality between heaven and earth.

Yeshua knelt on the sand so he was nearer Heron's height. He stretched out his hand and held it a few inches from her heart. He smiled gently. Her face was alight and receptive, open and innocent. No words were spoken, but, in her heart, she felt she carried a blessing that all would be well.

Mariam ushered her back into the tent to prepare for their journey. As Heron gathered her blankets in her arms, she watched Mariam scoop the string of brown-black beads and green stones. She watched as she slipped them down the front of her robe, inside some undergarment, where they nestled safely against her heart. Mariam looked fondly at the girl and her look of love seemed to reactivate Yeshua's blessing in her heart that everything would be alright.

Together, they walked in the scrubby landscape. A man was with them. He wasn't one of the people who had sat around the fire with Yeshua the previous night. He was with them to take care of things. The tents, the provisions, the animals. He was silent, too, but not like her silence, she thought. His silence was a withholding, a bitterness, born of an unexpressed hurt to which he righteously clung, not wanting to engage with these people for whom he worked.

After some time, a river stretched before them. Heron knew it must be crossed. It was fast-moving. The sun shimmered on the ever-changing surface as it twisted and eddied between the rocks that protruded and dictated the shape of the surging waters. Heron stood at a loss. She listened to its noise and felt the river's power impacting her senses.

From the bank, Heron watched as the man led and the donkey followed. The animal picked its way through the waters, stumbling over the unseen bed of the river. Heron could gauge the water's depth. The donkey's load shifted alarmingly, but the animal was adept and it held steady. It emerged on the opposite side, following what appeared to be a well-worn and familiar pathway trodden into the bank. Heron felt heartened that this must be a well-used crossing point. And there they stood on the far bank, the man and the laden donkey, waiting.

The surging river reminded her of the currents she knew beneath the Earth. In her mind's eye, she saw again the coursing, molten, liquid electricity moving in some uncontrolled, random, unpredictable way through subterranean channels in a surge of endless variants. She had an understanding that this was not random to Mother Earth. Mother knew what she was doing with her energy currents. And as Heron faced the seething torrent of the river, she took a leap of trust that as below, so above and that this river, too, knew what it was doing, as some expression of Mother's wisdom.

Suddenly, Mariam was at her side. "Our turn," she said and took Heron's hand. In a leap of faith, Heron allowed herself to be pulled into the water.

She put her trust in the hand of Mariam around her own and in her surrender, the woman of Mariam seemed to blend with the woman of Mother Earth through the medium of Mother's waters. Mariam, Heron, the river. All three became one. Heron fixed her eyes ahead on the donkey, not the river, and somehow her foothold was strong and the rocks beneath supported her and opened up a pathway to the other side. She and Mariam emerged. A smile and a look were held between them of a growing trust.

10

Heron was confronted with increasingly loud, harsh sounds. She held tightly to Mariam's hand as she led her into the hustling and bustling of some busy marketplace or town. People shouted. There was so much shouting. They looked different; they spoke differently. Animals were braying; squawking chickens were flapping and flustering as a boy poked them along with a long stick. This was all an assault on Heron's senses. She lowered her head to try and stop the sights and sounds coming in. Chin tight on her chest, she watched her own feet pick through the dust and droppings. Dirt was scratching in her lungs, choking smells of acrid meat scorching on fires. She felt as if she were being pummelled, battered and she braced herself against it.

Heron had woken this morning in the peace of the desert, companionably with Mariam at her side. The rhythm of their travels, their quietness and ease were a balm to her. She had felt untroubled. And this was their destination? Was this where it was all leading? It was almost unbearable to contemplate that their peaceable travels had led to this.

Perhaps she had expected to arrive in some oasis, some blissful physical reflection of the calm inner world she had been inhabiting with Mariam these last few days. A eutopia, a heaven on earth place to match her deep sense of inner belonging. A place where she would be as at ease outside as she was inside. This was no such place. She had never seen so many people. Beggars, people bandaged in rags where limbs should be, the corpse of a dog alive and seething with flies. Mariam held her hand tightly and moved her as fast as she could through the cacophony, the hustling of life scrapping to survive.

They broke away down a side alley. Heron had never been beside buildings so high that the sun wasn't able to penetrate in any direct way. It was like stepping into a cool and shaded tunnel. With each step between her and the marketplace, her body relaxed and her delicate nerves seemed to rearrange themselves again into a more comfortable order.

It was quiet here, only their footsteps echoed up the walls of the alleyway. Mariam slowed them down to a more relaxed pace and they walked until the buildings became less and the spaces became more. Then, Mariam stopped. She knelt down next to Heron and took both of her hands. Heron knew she was going to say something unwelcome, something she didn't want to hear, and her senses were on alert in some heightened, anxious anticipation.

Mariam spoke gently, "My child. You and I have come a long way together. But now it is time for us to part. I have brought you to this special place. Behind these gates, you will feel safe. Inside, there are only women. Women who devote their lives to the mysteries of the universe. They are like us. We are all the same in that we have knowledge of some very special mysteries. The secrets of the stars and their magical connection to all that is on this earth."

Heron was stunned. She sensed she was meant to be beguiled by this information, but she could barely hear it. All she felt was the pull in her heart that Mariam was about to leave her.

"It's alright, my child." Mariam held the girl in her heart and continued, "You will be safe here. Work hard, learn everything, be a keen and obedient scholar."

Heron didn't want this; she didn't want to be left in this strange and frightening town. Her heart was sinking. Mariam opened the gate from the street into an inner courtyard. Here, the air felt calm and Heron could hear running water somewhere, though as she looked around the orderly layout of things, she could not see its source. Maybe it was just the air that felt soothing like running water. Mariam ushered her in.

They walked together across the courtyard. Heron holding Mariam's hand just a little tighter now. Mariam led her towards a large, wooden door, much bigger than the first gate. An entrance to a large stone building. They stopped in front of it and Heron looked at the carvings on the door; she didn't know what they meant. Mariam lowered her gaze and knelt at the wide stone step before it. Heron knew to follow her lead and she knelt down obediently on the ground beside her. Mariam lowered her head to the stone step. Heron followed and, in the bowing, with their foreheads on the step, they seemed to merge with the energy of the stone, with the stone building. Mariam, Heron and the building all connected and alive and synchronised in her awareness. The sun baked down on their backs. Heron was aware of the sun like a hand pressing between her shoulders. Like a welcome; a solemn and sincere greeting. It felt kind and fatherly.

There was a hollow carved into the step, forming a kind of dish. It contained gold coins. They glistened in the sun, at odds with the dirty poverty of the rabble she had seen outside. Just there, this gold, so close to the poverty, but unseen by it.

And yet, Heron knew the gold was safe there. Anyone who came to this place would not take it; they sought other riches. Mariam opened her free hand and in it was another gold coin.

She handed it to the girl with the confidence that the child would understand its meaning. Heron took the coin and held it against her chest. Her heart instantly opened with the expansive love that resided within her. The love that guided and comforted her. She held onto this inner connection to her own heart and felt its permanence, its eternity, its infinity. Dwelling in this infinite expansion made her fearful attachment to Mariam now feel tight and hollow. And with that remembering of what she had within, she let go of Mariam's hand. And she found that her inner strength did not desert her. She placed the gold coin in the carved dish, an offering to the portal before her, and the strength in her heart burgeoned into courage to face what lay behind these doors.

Mariam stepped back. She knew the girl had accepted the invitation, the mission. Heron didn't notice Mariam leave. Her heart was already connected to what lay inside this building.

11

Heron woke up on a raised bed made of wood. She looked up at the walls around her. In daylight, she could see they were a soft, golden, sandy stone. She stood up. Folded at the end of her bed, she noticed a tunic. It was dark blackish blue in colour. She had never worn anything of this colour, but she knew to put it on. It would be her uniform. It made her think of Mariam's dark robes. Heron was nervous, but a deeper trust kept her steady. As she slipped the tunic over her head, she felt as though she was becoming encased in a new layer. Not just a layer of new fabric, but a new layer of some, as yet, undiscovered connection. Another layer of belonging to something but she didn't know what. She smoothed the front of the tunic down and rested her hands on her lower belly. Her ten-year-old womb seemed to activate and resonate with this new layer of mystery that this tunic represented.

She tidied her bed and felt the approach of someone, though she could hear no footsteps. She stood in readiness, facing the doorway. A wave of familiar kindness and ease touched her senses and her heart yielded. This loving wave preceded the physical form, who then appeared in the doorway.

Mariam stood smiling at her. Heron knew in that loving gaze that Mariam had tested her faith the day before on the steps.

Mariam needed Heron to walk into the unknown relying on her own faith and not at the behest of another. Heron had been prepared to leave Mariam and so now they met anew. Heron no longer felt the fond and clinging attachment to her that she had felt on the journey here.

She regarded Mariam now with a new freedom in her heart, a spaciousness free from her reliance, her subtle need of Mariam. A new level of connection seemed to have been opened between them. More balanced, more equal. And she knew that Mariam had left the folded tunic at the end of her bed as a symbol of this. Together, they stood in understanding, eyes merging and hearts smiling.

Mariam's face broke into a wide, soft smile, which showered Heron with her fondness. "Come along then," she said. "We have work to do."

And this time, Heron walked beside her, but did not need to hold her hand.

They walked into a vast chamber. It felt simple, pure and clear. Heron's eyes scanned up the high, plain walls. Her neck craned to reach the top. The chamber was cool and swept clean. There were women moving about the periphery, quietly getting on with whatever they had to do. A woman walked through, carrying armfuls of crumpled fabric as if she would launder it in some other place. Elsewhere, she heard the distant echoing laughter of women.

The chamber was cool and dim and gentle on her senses. A pool of light brightened the stone floor. From its circular shape and defined edges, she imagined the light must be admitted through an aperture in the ceiling, for there were no windows to be seen in the walls of this large and simple space. But somehow, she found she could not look up towards the aperture to confirm her theory and instead kept her gaze on the pool of light it cast upon the ground.

Mariam could feel that the girl had sensed the importance of the pool of sunlight. They stood side by side at the edge of the illuminated circle cast upon the floor. Mariam knelt down and Heron obeyed her silent directive to follow. She mirrored Mariam's solemn supplication before the pool of sunlight. Heron felt the nature of the energy in this shaft of light emanating from above. A fatherly space, safe, strong, like the hand of the sun she had felt on her back, welcoming her as she had knelt on the step the day before.

In silent prayer, Mariam surrendered herself to the sunlight space, making herself nothing in her bowing before it. Heron felt all this and she shed her own nerves and placed her trust in this masculine field of light, which gently illuminated the otherwise unlit chamber.

They stood and, together with solemn reverence, stepped into the centre of the pool of light. Heron could feel that the sun was not directly overhead, but in her mind's eye she saw the first burning fronds of the corona, cresting the edge of the opening in the roof. His fiery fingers creeping towards it like the unstoppable, creeping, searing edge of a magma flow.

Mariam turned and faced the girl. A woman in a dark robe kneeling opposite a girl in a dark tunic in a pool of sunlight. Their eyes connected. Heron saw a deep, shifting, purple black void in Mariam's eyes and sank deeply into it. Once Mariam knew this had been recognised and connected to, she reached into her robes and pulled out the string of dark beads and green stones that she had carried with her in the desert. She cupped them in both hands. Heron's eyes were closed. She was deep in the womb-like blackness, sunken into her downstairs home through the depths of Mariam's eyes. Mariam deftly twisted the string of beads in her fingers and looped it into a particular shape. With both hands, she held open the loop and placed it upon her own head. It sat like a circle on her hair, making a ring, a wreath, a crown on her brow.

"My child." She spoke to call Heron back to awareness. And Mariam held the girl steady in her heart as she instructed her to slowly open her eyes. Before Heron's eyes could focus properly, she felt the pulsing of something between her eyes. And she sensed the string of beads around Mariam's head. She wasn't sure if her eyes were open or closed, but she saw a large green gemstone hung on Mariam's forehead, centrally above her eyes. The green stone was alive and suddenly sending its power across to Heron. She held steady, rooted in the black void, as this cosmic stone delivered its load between her eyes and down through her heart and womb space to the great womb of Mother.

Heron waited and waited deep in her darkness. Slowly, Mother's womb began to return an energy. It spiralled slowly up from the depths, coiling around her spine on its ascent, breaking to dust anything on its route, leaving a crystalline spiral pathway in its wake.

The rising energy met Heron's heart and swirled around it and through it in a green swimming light. It infused her heart with emerald-green light, billowing, shifting until it felt as if her heart were saturated, replete. Her heart felt like a sponge, waterlogged with green light, heavy, saturated and only just holding its shape, and should a finger touch it, the green light would leak down the finger of the toucher, down their hand and down their arm and into their own heart.

As Heron's eyes slowly focused, she saw that the green jewel that hung on Mariam's brow was the shape of a heart. Her inner vision showed her how the shape of the heart was constructed. An infinity symbol, like a figure of eight, lay on its side along the top, forming the two upper lobes of the heart. A black dot marked the intersection point at the middle of the infinity symbol. The place of perfect balance, a null point, a place where infinity becomes nothingness.

In her inner vision, two lines came down from the widest sides of the infinity symbol, in symmetry, coming together as if to focus the whole of infinity in one spot. The point at the bottom of the heart shape. This, too, was marked with a black dot. Two black dots. The black dot of no-thing above the black dot of every-thing below. The symbol of the potential of the human heart. Infinite creation from the pure potential of nothingness. The template that resides in every human heart.

She let the green heart fade away. She had understood its meaning and it became again just a green stone in a string of beads.

It was done. Mariam helped the girl to her feet and they stepped outside the pool of light, just as the sun crept over the rim of the aperture and flooded the darkened chamber with its glorious, warm, golden rays. They stood and watched the shimmering golden sunlight bless the chamber, touching its very darkest depths. And they bowed to his majesty, his glory, his bringing of life, his providence, his bestowing, delivering, blessing.

12

As dusk was falling, Heron found herself back in the chamber. She had wandered there by herself. She wanted to revisit the place. It held a mystery for her; unknown but important. Her experience earlier had touched her deeply, but was beyond what her mind could comprehend.

She stood looking at the pale circle upon the floor. As the day was ending, the power she had felt in the shaft of light was now just a remnant of the strength it conveyed earlier. Just a lingering reminder of its capacity.

Slowly, as she waited, the chamber gradually fell into total darkness. Without the light, without this masculine presence infiltrating the chamber, it was returned to the still blackness of the feminine. A patient receptivity was in the air. A contentment, a satisfaction. As if the chamber itself were a womb with an opening in the ceiling to receive the masculine. She felt some deep understanding of the relationship between the masculine and the feminine embed into her. A knowing of the sacred union of all creation.

She took this knowing with her and she returned to lay on her wooden bed. She fell easily into a dream-filled sleep. She dreamed of all of the stars in the universe. Each star another burning sun. Billions of them, each with a message, a spark, a flint, a crack, a sound, a perfect and beautiful gift. Stars waiting, ready and eager to serve the great womb of Mother Earth, to give her that for which she longs, to initiate her perfect creations.

In her dream, Heron floated among the stars. The Gods were giving her a guided tour through a feast of available sparks. Choose this, choose that, an introduction to all the possibilities, just there, strong, ready to serve. Each sun bowed to her as she passed it by. And, in return, she bowed to them. Her heart filled with reverence for these kings of the firmament. And they bowed deeply to their queen, prostrating themselves at her feet, bowing to the mystery within woman, which they did not understand but would give their lives for. She gave them purpose, meaning, a vehicle for their highest expression. And she knew, too, that the womb she was carrying through the firmament would remain just empty potential without the divine spark, the masculine arrow, the balance. And she floated in the harmony of this mutuality. The beautiful electric poise; the precision of their opposite requirements of the other to express their own, each other's and their combined possibility.

She drifted into a deeper sleep, cushioned by an inner comfort that held her through the night.

She was woken at dawn by the sounds of women chattering and beginning their domestic tasks. She felt peaceful and clear. She opened her eyes. The sun had returned and penetrated the darkness of her room and a new day was born.

13

Mariam stood in the doorway. "I am going to show you something today. Come, child."

Heron was ready in her dark tunic, pleased to see Mariam and ready for the day. The days seemed to unfold in this place as if to some plan – some preordained, already written plan for her. Heron was happy with this. It was like stepping onto a moving conveyor. She was obedient, trusting and courageous, and she was willing to step into this moving current, this flow of things.

Together, they walked out into the courtyard she had seen on her arrival. There were many orderly beds of plants. The beds were laid out in pleasing regular patterns. The plants looked carefully placed and well-tended. They seemed to almost speak to her. They seemed alive, animated and busy being whatever they were.

They seemed to have voices, personalities, unseen female presences. A tendril stroked her leg as she passed, yet she was not close enough for its physical fronds to touch her. It was like walking through a strange wonderland of unseen women. She could think of no other description. They smiled at her, welcomed her, approved of her and almost ushered her along, spinning and weaving some invisible mesh around her. It made the girl smile inside. They were loving, encouraging, motherly, sisterly; a mystical sorority of plants. It was enchanting and Heron's heart felt light with excitement. Mariam could feel the girl's connection to the garden as she hoped she would. The girl was ready.

At the far edge of the garden was another entranceway and they turned to face it. Two trees stood, one either side of the portal. Mariam paused and took an audible breath as if to centre herself and acknowledged the trees. Without words, they descended a stone staircase towards the darkness. Heron ran her hand down the stone wall to steady herself as her eyes adjusted to the diminishing light. They stood before a door, lit dimly by the remains of the light that reached it.

Mariam unlocked the door and pushed it open. Heron was hit by a pungent, heady aroma, which seemed to permeate all her senses. Mariam lit a lamp and then another, and gradually from the darkness emerged the detail of the room before her. It was not large and a table or bench against the wall seemed to occupy a large part of it. She could see paraphernalia, small things, items she did not recognise. Vials, jugs, containers of various sizes, strange-shaped glass objects, tools and dishes. Some kind of workbench. Mariam let the girl take in the room. After a few moments, she spoke, "What is it, my child? Go to it; go to what is calling you."

Heron stepped forwards and slowly trailed her hand over a long row of jars and vials of different shapes and sizes, each with a symbol inscribed upon it. Her fingers hovered over the jar that was reaching out, as if a woman was beckoning from within it, with a warm familiarity that Heron heard with her heart. Mariam encouraged her silently to pick up the small, bulbous clay jar. It nestled in her cupped hands close to her chest and it made Heron feel something that she felt in Mariam and her own mother – an unconditional love and holding. She was suddenly anxious. Was it possible to distil this feeling into something that could be contained in a vessel? That is how it felt to her as she stood in the flickering half-light with this potion encapsulated in the clay and the clay cupped in her palms.

"Come, bring her with you," said Mariam. And now the selection was made, they left the room and reascended the staircase back into the daylight. Heron followed Mariam through the gardens, but instead of returning to the building she knew, they went towards the gate to the outside alleyway. Mariam held the gate open, not engaging with Heron's questioning eyes, as the girl stepped through with both hands still holding the small stoppered jar. Heron knew her obedience was required, so trusted both Mariam and the woman in the jar, both of whom did not share her anxiety. They seemed unconcerned and matter of fact about what lay ahead.

Instead of turning towards the marketplace, Heron was relieved to find they walked in another direction. It led them through streets and alleyways, up steps, through patches of trees and between dwellings. Mariam clearly had a destination in mind, and the jar in Heron's hands felt as though she knew where she was going and what her mission was, too. Heron allowed herself to be shown, guided by the two assured female presences.

They stopped at the entrance to a dwelling. Mariam called inside in the language Heron did not understand. The language of this town. Heron held the jar as if it might break, like a warm and fragile egg in her hands; the chick inside fully grown and about to break its way out – ready, alive, its moment. She just had to hold onto it and keep it safe a little while longer.

Voices inside beckoned and they entered the dwelling. It was simple but cared for. There were jars of fresh water and it had the soft feel of a well-tended home. But there was tension in the faces of the two women who greeted them. Mariam spoke with them.

Heron surveyed the room and, with an inner jolt, she noticed a raised bed arrangement in one corner with a person laying in it. A very small person, a very old person. As she registered this, Mariam moved over to the bed and gently smoothed the blanket and touched the backs of her fingers lightly on the person's sunken temples. Heron was rooted to the spot and held the pulsing jar against her heart.

Mariam's gaze called her over and Heron sat beside her in front of the person in the bed. The air suddenly took on a holy, expanded reverence, through which Heron vaguely heard Mariam explain that the woman was the mother of the two women. That her time was near; she would leave her body soon, the end of her encasement, and she would return home.

Heron could see the old woman's chest rising. Her eyes were closed and mouth half open, strung with mucus through which her lungs heaved a heavy breath, which tenuously sustained her. Heron could also see the fine energy filaments. All that was left holding this woman in her casing. The body was no longer needed and it was shutting down in readiness for the release. The dense energies of her body were now overshadowed by the woman's expanding spirit.

Heron had not seen a dying person before. But the natural tenderness of her heart opened and she connected easily to the figure crumpled and wasted before her. The woman's bones protruded visibly as if to loudly declare their presence. First formed as the spirit entered the foetus in the womb decades before and laying mostly hidden beneath the flesh in life, and now starkly revealing themselves. The bones felt significant; a silent inner framework, a hidden scaffolding for a physical body, and it seemed to represent the hidden inner scaffolding Heron sensed within herself, the inner crystalline framework that gave her strength through her connection to the divine, the universal source.

Mariam nodded to the jar and smiled. "You chose correctly. This holy oil called out to you as it can help with the mission today. You heard its cry. Listen to her now. She will help carry this woman across the veil to glimpse the paradise beyond, to comfort her, to alleviate her fear of what awaits."

The old woman of bones lay with her jaw hanging, her breath labouring in some relentless, struggling rhythm of life.

Mariam continued, "You are holding the spirit of the nard. She is distilled from the core of the spikenard plant and she is held in the oil. She is a beautiful mistress. Let her guide you."

Heron sat with the remnants of a physical life, still held by fibres to the bones in front of her. The woman in the jar of nard wanted to come out. Heron obeyed her. She held the jar over her heart and pulled out the stopper. The oil's vapour rose in a pungent cloud, engulfing her, and she breathed it in. As she inhaled the rich mysterious particles, she became one with them. The woman of the spikenard guided her hand and Heron held the jar a few inches above the dying woman. Starting above her head, she dragged the jar and its trail of vapours through the fine filaments of the woman's aura. It coated her in a deep swirling aliveness, which seemed to rise and expand through the grid of all dimensions – the grid of everything in Heron's inner vision.

The girl's eyes were closed and her womb pumped upwards as if Mother Earth herself was pushing the nard and some fluid aspect of the dying woman out into the everything. Heron's heart held everything safe, like a container for it all. And she sat like this with infinite patience and trust, just being as wide and solid, as unbreakable and timeless as a canyon. The nard lifted the fine delicateness of the woman into realms unseen, as her body lay on the bed, her chest still rising and falling, working hard, labouring.

After some minutes, Heron felt the nard withdraw. The woman of the nard bowed in gratitude to her and the girl inwardly bowed in return and replaced the stopper in the jar. The vapours were finished and Heron put the jar to one side.

Heron was deeply touched by this dance with the divine, this privilege, this responsibility. Her mind couldn't begin to encompass it, but to her heart it was beautiful. A most beautiful way to connect with other humans around whom she usually felt so awkward and at odds.

She reached forward and took the hand of bones, rigid and crooked beneath a wafer of skin, which she felt might tear with her touch. She needed to touch this person. Heron was filled with awe and wonder and wholeness at the union she had felt with the everything, and she hoped and wondered whether the woman had shared the experience with her.

At her touch, the woman opened her glassy eyes. And although they looked too cloudy to see through, from them emanated a gaze of such deep, all-encompassing peace, such completeness, as if she had been shown a glimpse of her own perfection and the perfection of everything. There was no fear in her eyes, just love – a reflection of the love that is the everything. A reflection of the love she had felt. A love that had seen her, recognised her, soothed her and to which she knew she would soon return. The love of home. The nard had taken her there, bridged the veil, the divide between bones and no bones.

Heron sat for several hours, the woman's hand laying in hers. Gradually, the woman's breathing relaxed, became shallower and the pauses between the breaths lengthened. The air changed – it became bright and pixelated and billowed softly like a heat haze – and Heron watched the fine filaments detaching from the woman. A fine gossamer cobweb of silky fibres gathered and moved at the same time from her feet and her head, hovering over her form and gathering at the centre, spinning together in a beautiful white cord reaching upwards. Her aliveness left through some unseen umbilical and returned to whence it came.

In the silence, tears rolled gently down Heron's cheeks. Not of sadness, but of wonder and humility. She felt infinitesimally small; she felt like nothing in the enormity of that which she had touched. And in being nothing, she was everything.

14

On the floor of her room, Heron noticed a beetle. She knew it was dead. It had lost its lustre. A corpse, its spirit departed, a husk. She thought of the woman the day before who had died and she thought of the spikenard. The beetle was the size of the top part of her thumb. She picked it up and turned it in her hands, thinking of the perfection of the process. The life, the maintenance, the death, the cycle. As she pondered, some part of her seemed to connect to the life that had been in the beetle. She knew it still existed, just that it was somewhere else in the endless grid of everything. It seemed to expand in her awareness, the aliveness of the beetle, but separate from the corpse in her hand. As if she held them both somehow.

Mariam appeared at the door as usual to collect her for the day's instruction. Heron was pleased to see her. She was nourished by this place, by this woman. The inner world she had held like a precious secret was now expressed, spoken to, enriched here in this learning place with Mariam, whose purpose in being there, it seemed to Heron, was solely to guide and teach her. To see the fullness of her, to impart wisdom and to reflect her own gifts back to her, gradually empowering the girl to uncover them and use them wisely and skilfully, with discernment and the utmost integrity.

Mariam looked at the beetle that lay in Heron's open palm. She read the girl's mind, travelled the same thoughts and smiled at her. "Come with me, and bring your friend." And she glanced at the lifeless shell.

Today, they did not eat breakfast. They just drank water, which left a trace of some mineral on Heron's lips. It was not the same as water fresh from a well or a spring. But it satisfied her body, and her lips liked the taste of the salty mineral. They sat in silent meditation together for several hours.

By the middle of the day, Heron was empty. Empty of thoughts and empty of food, but full of divine spaciousness. Together, she and Mariam entered the great chamber with the pool of light upon the floor. Everything felt more heightened than the last time. Her senses, inward and outward more piqued, more acute, more highly tuned. Mariam took her to the edge of the chamber where the walls met the floor and showed her the scuttling beetles, the living expression of the dead friend she held in her hand.

Again, the creeping corona of the sun was close to the opening in the roof. With the same ritual reverence as before, they knelt before the shaft of sunlight, surrendering to his majesty. They stepped into the centre of the circle and knelt opposite one another. Mariam produced the string of beads from her robes and this time she looped them ceremonially around Heron's head, as if coronating her with a sacred crown. The heart-shaped emerald gemstone hung over the girl's brow.

Heron could barely feel her physical body. It was as if she was completely inhabiting the invisible part of herself – the enormous, never-ending part at one with the great love. There was no time, there was nothing – it felt – keeping her in this body, but she trusted a few tendrils must remain binding her to the stone floor.

Mariam spoke, "The only man who is permitted in this temple is the sun." And they waited. Heron could feel the impending arrival of the man as his warm rays began to overspill through the aperture in the ceiling. His power increased moment by moment as he passed overhead until he shone his full dynamic magnificence down upon her. A roaring power consumed her, invigorating her as she reverberated in this moving column of light particles. The green jewel above her eyes started to activate. Her physical eyes blinked tighter, stretching and flickering behind their closed lids.

She heard Mariam's voice, "Take the beetle in your hand and lift it to the sun."

Heron felt for the lifeless beetle and moved it from her palm to her fingers and, with both hands, lifted it high. So doing, she craned her neck up to the opening and the downward penetrating surge of sunlight. A cosmic light came through her, rattling her hands, her brow, her heart and came to rest in her womb space.

With her own inner vision, Mariam was observing the movement of the Light within her pupil. "Use your woman," she instructed. And Heron shifted her focus to the downstairs, her womb, Mother Earth's womb and the Light followed her attention and pumped downwards through her. And she was held in the safe, encircling embrace of the masculine sunlight, in the reverberating stillness.

Heron lowered her arms and intuitively held the beetle in her hands over her heart. Then, she sensed a tenderness beyond compare. She felt a mother's love for her own creation wash through her. Mother Earth loved this beetle with a magnitude of tender care that was nearly overwhelming to the girl. Mother Earth knew the value of its place in the tapestry of her impeccable creation of all life. The beetle was of the utmost importance, as great and vital and loved as any being. With this, Mother sent a spiralling life force energy back up through the girl. Her pure and open heart received it and transferred it through her hands, with a love so complete, so perfect, so intended for this sacred creature.

And all became still. After some moments, Heron slowly opened her eyes. She was aware of Mariam opposite. The circle they knelt in was bright. And she gradually returned to a more earthly awareness and they knelt together in stillness.

In her balled hands, Heron felt the movement of life. Her heart rose. She lifted her head and shot an excited look at Mariam. Mariam smiled broadly. Heron was suddenly filled with childlike excitement and she lifted one hand away to reveal the beetle cupped in the other. Shiny and black, purposeful, resplendent in its glistening armour, antennae searching and legs twitching. Heron was overspilling with joy. Her eyes brimming with the innocence of the child that she was, and she grinned in delight and amazement at her teacher.

The beetle was off, crawling up her arm. Heron jumped and flicked it onto the floor and it scuttled out of the bright sunlight into the darker reaches of the chamber. Part of the girl wanted to follow it, play with it, have the extraordinary moment acknowledged between them. But Heron knew her part was done and that she had no hold on the beetle's life. It owed her nothing.

Instead, Heron sat looking into the eyes of her teacher. No words came from her mouth, but she conveyed to Mariam a deep gratitude, for her, for the beetle, for it all. And as Mariam's love reflected back to her and held her, Heron's lip trembled and it seemed as though some inner rose in her heart had opened another petal, which could never be closed again.

15

Many days had passed in this building. It allowed her to feel more complete and at one with herself. This temple without, like her temple within. Her days were spent with Mariam and her nights with her dreams. She had uncovered layers of herself. Layers of her inner world, which allowed her to overlap ever further with the grid of everything. Her heart was strong, a courage swelled. A courage to know the glory of her own sovereignty, through the dissolution of her fears. She knew about the firmament, about star systems, galaxies, and understood their celestial medicine for Mother Earth and her children. For all living things.

She travelled in her dreams and watched her own mother at the well, busy with other women and children, but alone inside. Heron sent waves of love to the woman who she loved for letting her go. She missed her mother's warm softness, her smile, her touch, their ways. Their love bridged everything. These were warm dreams, comforting dreams, and she knew that everything would be alright. And she poured her love into the wrenching twists in the cord between them when they arose.

Heron sensed her time here was nearing its end. She had grown in her inner authority, her agency over who she really was. She had faith in her abilities and gifts and in her unusual ways. She now accepted herself as she had been accepted here. A solid foundation had been cemented within her, reinforcing her inner skeleton of strength. Her bones were stronger; they became an anchor. The bony framework within was a template, a pattern, a blueprint of her more nebulous, fluid aspects. The anxiety that once held her in a kind of straitjacket had been transformed in her time here into something healthier, made roomier from love.

Heron had the impending sense that things were about to change. And so, Mariam appeared in the doorway of her room and announced just that. "It is time for us to leave," she said. "Look at you," and she beamed, appreciating this subtle yet important transformation in the girl. "I will travel with you. Everything is ready. We will return to Yeshua."

Heron's world spun with excitement, a deep glow grew within as she remembered this man, who was unlike anyone she had encountered. With whom she felt special and cherished and whose touch, whose look, seemed to activate all that was good in her.

Heron was ready. There was no hesitation. She turned and thanked the room in silent gratitude for housing her, for she knew she would not see it again. The stone walls nodded their acceptance and seemed to blow a gentle breeze carrying her out into the unknown, filling her sails with good wishes.

There were no other goodbyes, not to the women and not to the man from the roof opening. There was a sense of purpose in Mariam, an urgency almost. Heron could feel an apprehension arising in her teacher, a trepidation, a sense of duty, or necessity about this journey back to her beloved husband. This unease, she sensed, was born of her commitment and loyalty to him and their unbreakable bond. Heron saw two ships tossing on a stormy sea, in peril, but the rope between them held fast. They were conjoined, inseparable. Heron had a reverence for

Mariam and a respect for the situation she sensed. A challenging situation; Mariam and Yeshua bound together in hostile waters, facing difficult decisions. Mariam inextricably bound, it seemed, to whatever unfolded around Yeshua, or with what events the Light of Yeshua attracted to it.

Mariam barely spoke and nodded the briefest greeting to a man who stood harnessing donkeys. Mariam lifted the girl on to one of them without a word about their mission, without any of her usual kind words. She was distracted, deep in thought. The man led a donkey heavily laden with provisions for what Heron supposed would be a long journey. Mariam walked separately from them. She was solemn, her heart heavy, like a weight suspended, swinging with every step, held steady within a strong mesh of fibres of dignity and courage.

Heron responded with respect and acceptance and trust. As the donkey pitched and swayed beneath her, she watched the arid land pass by around her. The trees were thinning now as the scrubby terrain gradually gave way to desert. The trees became increasingly scraggy and desiccated, taken to the edge of their lives by the baking sun. Not lush and verdant, quite the opposite, dry and wizened but still with life. The leaves were more grey than green, yet the trunks were old and twisted so they must have thrived for years, growing bent against the heat and prevailing winds, she imagined. Even the trees did not seem to want to communicate, as if everyone sensed something too unnerving to put into words. It felt a long journey without Mariam's companionship. But the girl was accepting, allowing it all.

They stayed in dwellings along the way. Mariam seemed to know the people. Heron heard them talking in hushed tones late into the night as she lay in another room, sleep evading her. She was excluded from their conversations. She knew it was not her place. But Mariam could not exclude her from the transmissions of discord and anxiety that pervaded the atmosphere.

Heron succumbed to sleep and spent an uneasy, fitful night. In her dreams, she saw ravens – big black birds with shiny eyes as hard as glass beads. Sharp black pointy beaks. The ravens were pecking at a carpet, a rug, woven of the finest silk threads. A precious and fine interweaving of intricacy and beauty. Peck, peck, peck until holes appeared and the strength of the weave was corrupted by the vulgar intrusion. Peck, peck, peck. Dark, unthinking automatons, operating from some primal mechanical instinct to peck. Their claws dug into the weave, black beaks pecking, pecking, pecking, ignorant in their destruction.

16

Yeshua stood outside with his group of itinerant men; the same men that had been gathered around the fire. They stayed close to him. Together, they had been travelling to settlements, staying on the fringes and drawing the local people to them. It was Yeshua they came to listen to. He uplifted them with his words. He instructed them and they listened, eager for something he had. As if he gave them an answer to their troubled ways of being. He was assertive. He spoke forcefully. His message powered forth with an intensity that arrested the people gathered to listen. Some wandered away fearfully and others were beguiled by this man. His words carried a Light, with a force that pierced some long-forgotten remembrance held deep within them. This was his mission. To waken the eternal truth within each man and woman. To awaken the kingdom and queendom of heaven within them.

Crowds regularly gathered and word went ahead, preceding his movements, and so crowds were already waiting at the next neighbourhood. His pull on the townspeople did not go unnoticed by wider governance. But he was relentless in his messages to the people.

In spite of his close companions, Yeshua felt quite alone in his work, his mission. He drew comfort from his inner world.

He thought of Mariam, his pillar of strength, and with whom he shared his inner and outer world. There was a yearning in his heart. They were to be reunited soon. He looked to the horizon. She was coming.

Heron and Mariam were leaving the latest dwelling place. The women had been kind to Heron. They fed her and fussed fondly over Mariam's little travelling companion. They cupped her face with their hands and spoke good wishes. They chatted brightly, their faces smiling, but Heron knew they were employing some instinct to somehow protect or distract her from their real feelings, which she could tell were not so bright.

Mariam seemed more talkative after meeting with her friends, galvanised, more invigorated, and she spoke to Heron, "We have two more days to travel, my child. We will cross the desert and we will meet Yeshua." Heron quietly enjoyed this reaffirmation of their destination.

Mariam produced a length of fabric, which, with her direction, Heron wrapped around her head and face and shoulders as protection from the sun and desert winds. Mariam climbed up onto a camel and pulled the girl up in front of her. Heron scrambled onto the beast. A camel man mounted another and shouted commands at the animals, who lurched and unfolded. They set off, their camel trailing the one in front and their mounted guide as if an invisible coupling kept them all together.

Heron allowed herself to be held by Mariam. Wrapped in their scarves with just their eyes showing, it was easy to mistake them for one enshrouded person.

The journey was hard and the desert unforgiving. The joyful easy companionship and the sense of expectation of their first journey was replaced by a more solemn air. Heron allowed herself to be lulled by the rocking rhythm of the camel's gait and the embrace of Mariam and she drifted away into reverie.

Her dream returned. It troubled her. It felt foreboding. The ravens were circling overhead, gathering, scoping, watching, stony, focused, cold.

The travellers had covered many miles. In the distance, a town or settlement became visible and Mariam shouted to the camel man ahead of them for confirmation. He did not look back and shouted his monosyllabic response. They were almost there.

Heron could feel Mariam changing – from their travelling torpor to a rising nervous excitement. They were both looking forward to a reunion with Yeshua. Heron in a girlish way, keen to feel his appreciation and his special attention. For Mariam, there was a deeper pull in her heart. Her heart awaited its twin. The resonance of their two hearts pulling them back towards each other.

It was the end of the day as they approached the settlement. It was dimly glowing with lamps and fires and a thin moon shone her sliver of light from the heavens. There were voices, which rose to shouts. Heron knew the cries were connected to their arrival and, out of the dusk, a group of men stepped forward. There he stood. Yeshua was looking and smiling at the mummified cargo on the camel. His penetrating gaze was full of brightness and love and it cut through her tiredness and ignited her heart with a childlike glee.

The camel crumpled to the floor and Yeshua approached. Heron leaned forwards with her arms outstretched towards him, like a child greeted by its long-lost father. And Yeshua scooped her off the camel, swinging her around playfully, and placed her on the ground. How pleased she was to see him. His magic had run through her like a dazzling current and in that moment of his complete attention, she felt like his most treasured possession.

This memory warmed her later as she lay on her thin mattress in a dwelling house. This time, Mariam did not sleep beside her. She knew Mariam and Yeshua were becoming one again.

17

The following day, Yeshua and his group assembled outside. Heron hung her head low. She felt awkward and out of place with the group of adults around Yeshua in this strained atmosphere. They ignored her, their business too important for a child. They were earnest and she was unnoticed in the higher business at hand.

Heron stood with them, looking down at her feet. She distracted herself by examining them. She was wearing leather sandals that covered the soles of her feet, but the arrangement of straps allowed the sand and dust and dirt to ingress between her toes and across her feet in some silent and mystical migration of particles. She contemplated the dust stuck to her feet, outlining her toenails in a dark frame of dirt and grime.

Heron chewed her bottom lip. Her shoulder involuntarily contorted up to her ear as if her body were in a subtle recoil to this awkward situation.

As she slid a foot through the sand, contemplating the arc it made, she felt something on her back, coming in from a distance. A man's hand, but not with the fatherly welcome of the sun's hand she had felt as she arrived at the temple. The sense of this man's hand was unwelcome, unpleasant, laced with malintent. Her left shoulder lifted again in some involuntary protection and bracing against the intrusion of this hand.

It didn't go away. A man's eyes were locked on her from a distance, she could tell. And it was not the same way Yeshua had first singled her out with his eyes when he approached that day on the camel. This time, she was singled out by something, someone malevolent.

The adults – Yeshua, Mariam and their companions – became a sea of indistinguishable robes. One synchronised mass from which she was excluded. And now this presence was bearing down on her and she was alone with it. Some defiant part of her rose. A childlike, chin-jutting defiance, which was not going to cower and give away its power to the ominous presence. She girded herself, gathered her courage, and nobody noticed as she turned and faced this intruder head on.

She raised her head and met it squarely. There he was, in the distance, too far away to see his features, but his form was clear. He was one of the other people she saw around, dressed in a tunic of leather strips to his knees. He was a bully; she could feel it. Muscular, solid, heavy, unrefined, brutish and from him emanated a hunger for power, a domineering ruthlessness that frightened her.

She had seen the danger of men gripped by their own inner weakness, the magnitude of which reflected in their blind compulsion to dominate others. This man was awash with this toxic, dangerous combination. She could feel it sparking away inside of him. His inner calls of vulnerability and his response to it. Annihilate it. Inner annihilation, outer annihilation, as if his very survival depended on keeping his own inner frailty suppressed. And anything he encountered that reminded him of his vulnerability would be drawn into his pattern of suppression, dominance and annihilation.

She knew he was a dangerous man, and he was looking at her. He was looking at the group. His focus shifted to Yeshua. She read his thoughts. What power did this man have over the people? What power did this Yeshua have that he, himself, didn't? The merest acknowledgment that someone might be more powerful than him sent his frailty into a panicking frenzy within, and he raged against it. Raged against his inner vulnerability and raged against the influential man who had triggered it. He roared inside; I will have that power. He would take it and then how powerful would he be? The raging swirls of his imagined stolen power intoxicated him, engulfing him in a huge obliterating cloud of satisfying superiority, and it drowned out the fragile voice inside of him. Relief, a way forward, this was his way of being. He was ignorant to its mechanism, convinced by his power-hungry story as the key to his very survival. Heron could feel all of this emanating from the Roman on the hill.

Deep in their collective discussions, no one else had seen him. It was just her and the Roman. His eyes now bored directly into hers and she felt his desire to overpower her. Her small body braced. She stared. Her body quivered and she held fast. The Roman turned and disappeared over the brow of the hill. Heron felt sick in her stomach. A tight constriction gripped her, and the ravens in her mind circled tighter.

She stood, her heart beating loudly as she watched the adults. She was invisible to them. She could say nothing and she choked as her throat twisted. She wanted to warn them, to shout out, "Look! There's danger!" but the adults were unreachable, her voice severed. Tears pricked as she tried desperately to alert them to the danger, to force out a cry, but strangled filaments constricted and shrivelled in her throat and her heart broke for her own muteness.

18

eron was sitting cross-legged on a mattress on the floor of the room she had slept in that night. Absently, her fingers traced the contours of its surface. Mariam was distracted now, spending most of her time with Yeshua and their companions. She missed Mariam's close attention, her tutelage at the temple, their hours spent together and the time tending the women-plants in the garden.

Mariam had explained the gift of each plant. How the essence of them could be obtained through different and specific methods; extracted from the petals and leaves, the roots, the woody stems, the bark. Their spiritual essence could be released. The plants were happy to share it with Mariam, give themselves over to be harnessed in the pure oil from the olive trees, and to sit distilled into vials with their hearts open. They waited for a woman whose heart had similar resonant qualities and could lovingly and reverently connect to them, so they could merge and offer their wisdom and mystical gifts through her.

Heron spent many days with Mariam as she wove the spirits of the plants into the oils. And they would step forward at Mariam's request to assist with all manner of ills. Spiritual and emotional crises were illuminated with clarity and soothed, and so the suffering of people was alleviated.

Mariam had encouraged Heron in this learning and Heron was a keen student. The women of the oils, the spirits of the plants, loved the girl's integrity and innocence and they flowed easily through her. These were special moments for Heron. Merging with the heart of Mariam, attuning to her own deep connection with the plant spirits. It was an initiation over many days, attuning the girl, refining her intuition, grounding her confidence.

Heron remembered these times with fondness, when she shared an inner world with Mariam, but now she accepted that these moments were replaced. Mariam was preoccupied with other issues, with something pressing in the outer world.

Heron had been sitting alone for a long time while the adults talked in another room. She waited. She began to feel nervous. She was excluded from Mariam's inner world, which, only days ago, she had shared. She tried to calm herself with trust in a bigger picture, a plan that was beyond her comprehension. But it was difficult and her sense of unease was palpable.

Without warning, two men burst into the room. Heron was shot through with alarm. These were intruders, bad men, and as they stopped and fixed on her with the smirk of having achieved their objective, Heron knew she was their prey.

One of the men grabbed her and clamped his hand over her mouth, a filthy rank hand, pinching her face. In the same movement, he picked her up from behind and pinned her arms across her body with the grip of his other hand. Without a sound, he snatched her up and carried her. It was all so fast. A rag was forced into her mouth and tied tight, gagged around her head. It entangled with her hair, which twisted and pulled painfully in its knot. Her arms were bound around her and a sack came down over her head. Her senses were in shock. She froze in the face of the force used against her and she dropped to the ground inside the sack as its neck was drawn tightly closed.

She felt the man's grip around her middle as he lifted the sack under his arm and carried her away. It was done in seconds. Her mind was blank as the sack was thrown into a cart and it jerked into motion.

With the man's grip gone, her senses began to return, her feelings re-engaged and a corporeal panic kicked her breathing into action. Her heart was pounding and her body needed to gasp great lungfuls of air through her gagged mouth to meet its needs. She grappled for the air, desperately breathing in and out through her nose in some primitive survival activation beyond her control.

The bright sun penetrated the sacking and her body shook trying to find some inner balance in this vulgar assault of her senses. Her heart pounded in her chest; she clamped her eyes shut and concentrated on trying to breathe. The air that came in was thick and dusty from the sack, hot and rasping. She put all her focus on the in and the out, until some kind of a breathing balance was established. She held onto this pattern – in, out, in, out, in, out – as she rattled over rough ground to the gait of the animal pulling her. She latched onto the pattern of its steps. The pull, the release, the side-to-side roll, over and over. It gave her a framework, a rhythm, and her primal panic eventually gave way enough to allow her to make some kind of appraisal of her situation.

She knew this was very bad. Her insides twisted and she could feel the distance stretching between her and Mariam, lengthening with every rock of the cart. She sent out silent calls to Mariam – "Help me! Help me! Help me!" – pleading through the invisible strands that connected them. Her body hurt, her arms bound, she could not support her rocking body, which lurched and pitched at the mercy of the terrain.

The pain kept her in her body. There was no detaching from it as she seemed involuntarily focused on clinging to her corporeal state. Tears began to roll. Tears of shock, terror, helplessness, smallness.

She wanted Mariam; she wanted her mother. She wanted Yeshua to lift her in his arms and bring her out of this torment. She wanted his comfort, his safety, his strength. She held a thread to his heart and pleaded along it to be saved from this. Beseeching the strength of Yeshua like the Gods she had seen in her dreams, who would give their lives to serve her what she needed. To protect her vulnerability, her beauty, her mystery.

Where were the Gods of the heavens in the dark and violent malintent of these men who had taken her? She saw the light and dark of men. The capacity to uplift and exalt the feminine, the capacity to dominate and overpower it. All this in a man.

From the well of darkness she had been thrown into, her inner calls felt bleak and unheard. The adults were deep in their own troubles, absorbed, distracted, focused elsewhere, unreachable.

She rocked and she baked and her body jolted for what seemed like a very long time.

19

Heron stood on a cool, smooth, polished stone floor. Her sack casing had been removed, her arms unbound, her gag untied. The men had gone and she had been delivered to her destination.

She stood, bruised, disoriented and dishevelled, and she was facing a man. She steadied herself and tried to stay composed. But she recognised the dark brooding anger emanating from the man. He was the Roman on the hill, who had speared her as his prey with his eyes the day before.

Her heart was asphyxiated, a knot tightened and she stood frozen as he paced around before her. Below the leather sections of his tunic were legs as thick and powerful as tree trunks. Muscular and sun-baked, tense and taught. Even the hairs on them coiled tightly with some kind of pent-up possibility of detonation. Every fibre of him emitted a suppressed rage. He was a tinderbox. His arms were bulging and sinewy. His movements were somehow rigid, not fluid, as if they were dictated and constrained by his inflexible bulk. She did not look at his face. She was too frightened.

He called to a woman, who scampered from a side room. She brought water and silently tended to the girl. She offered water to Heron's lips, which she drank gladly. Heron tried to catch the eyes of the woman but they were downcast. She was under the control of the Roman, as terrified of him as she was herself. There was no relief or connection to be found with this woman. Heron searched urgently in her face for hope for her plight, but there was none.

The woman was a shell – part of her had left, it seemed. She bathed Heron's face. She dabbed the wet cloth on her arms where the ligatures had rubbed them red and sore. The cold water soothed Heron, the woman's attention was welcome, but she sensed it was just a stay of execution. The woman silently and mechanically continued to bathe her wounds as if she were using the act to try to hold back time, stretching it, before the girl's inevitable engagement with the pacing man. The man whose actions Heron suspected were responsible for the flight of life force from this woman, leaving her broken and empty.

His look towards the woman was of derision, disgust and contempt. His snarling dismissal sent her scurrying away. Something in Heron rose up, some part that knew he had stolen the woman's very essence. It was a theft that burned in her heart. The force of her inner anger surged up through her, raising her chin until it held firm and forward and galvanised her in some burning inferno of injustice at what had been taken from the woman. She felt all these injustices; the violent thefts of power, the brutality of the taking, the arrogant entitlement. The abuse of power. Dominant, violent, brutal, mindless, heartless. The furnace in her eyes met his.

His broad face was implacable. His eyes glared back, shallow, hard, impenetrable. Beneath his left eye, a jagged and discoloured scar sliced down the side of his face. It was glistening with a film of sweat and she detected the merest curl of his lip and a ruthless trace of delight at this engagement. His nostrils quivered almost imperceptibly as he breathed the air like an animal picking up the scent of its prey.

Her eyes matched his. Her inner power matching his outer power. Without taking his eyes off her, he slowly stepped forward, breathing heavily. Heron did not move; she could not move. She met his darkness with a simmering darkness of her own. The darkness and power of woman to destroy as she can create. She felt the power of Mother Earth like a volcano burning in her eyes as she glared into the man's unblinking eyes. Sweat beaded on his forehead. They were locked.

This was exquisite for the man. He allowed her challenge. It tasted delicious. An intoxication of this small girl's body and the challenge, the standoff, a chin-jutting holding off of his power. He allowed it. He enjoyed it. His body rushed with chemicals, swelling an intoxicating sense of his own power, swelling his manhood in an overwhelming rush of his own superiority and invincibility. The gaze continued. It was all Heron had. He delighted in his control, his mastery of each micromovement, his containment of this exquisite temptation. A trace of a smile, and a contemptuous laugh at her pathetic efforts at engagement.

The Roman leaned in, inches from her face. Her whole being and the full force of the currents of the great Mother beneath her surged through her. She became one with this stream; she entered into it. He lifted her tunic. Her heart roared like a volcano; she stood frozen and boiling. Body frozen but heart boiling as his breath moved across her face. He touched her. The volcano erupted and it was as if Mother Earth sent her roaring up into the heavens. From here, she looked down and watched as her own form disappeared from view, consumed by the raging monster, hammered into obliteration. His cargo of evil forced into every cell of her being. He wanted her Light, her power, but Mother Earth pushed it into safety and here it hung, looking down.

From up high, she looked down at her abandoned form laying on the floor, bleeding, broken, sobbing. She watched the man walk away, victorious. She watched the woman return with the water and bathe her and dress her and she watched her body stand up and walk out of the building in a trance.

Some remaining function guided her to a river, where she scrambled down its deep sides and crouched, lowering her wounds into the cool running waters. The waters streaked red as they ran beneath her. And she wept and wept at the pain, the violence, the horror. The water cleansed her wounds and she cried for her body, her friend.

She gathered leaves; the plants called out to her. She piled the broad leaves together and kneaded them in her hands and packed them like a poultice between her legs. She sat beneath a tree. She had never felt so desolate, so alone, so broken. Even the embrace of the tree went unnoticed.

And the broken-away part of herself stayed somewhere in the grid of everything, still connected to Heron by a thread. It would follow her around, but it knew it would not return until the girl was restored. This part of her would remain connected by a thread, the part of her full feminine power that had evacuated, that had left in that event. The rage, the power, the volcano would not return until it was safe to do so.

It might take many lifetimes before that part would feel the pull on its thread it had been waiting for. The time when it would be safe to return. In a time when a woman was safe. When it could return, unfearful of persecution, unafraid of destruction. The tug would come one day through the grid of everything and she would hear it. The highest, the fullest expression of the feminine would hear the call from the women below, calling it back home.

And it would return to its rightful place to bring wholeness; to where it could be reunited, embodied and expressed with no threat of persecution, violence, domination and destruction. It would return and it would be revered by the Gods, who had been waiting for the return of their Goddess. Waiting so that they can serve and protect the divine feminine and expand and be intoxicated by their own divine masculine power, their true power to which the Goddess willingly surrenders and freely gives her all.

20

Heron felt quite detached from things, separate, removed. There were people moving about before her, but she felt as though she were floating in a slightly altered state. She stood up and walked among them. She seemed to be invisible. No one noticed her. No one looked her way as she passed through them. Goats and sheep streamed across her path. The sounds of life and the people were muffled as if she, herself, were insulated by a layer of fleece, which diffused the world and protected her senses. She was glad to be invisible.

She wandered aimlessly. She was oblivious to the hands on her shoulders guiding her along. She just took one trance-like step after another. The thick wadding seemed to buffer her. It meant she felt nothing. She was distanced from the memory of her experience as she was held in her numbing blanket. It was better not to feel.

Like a shadow, she moved through the activities of the town, through the bustle of the people, animals, motion, commotion. On and on she walked. The hubbub faded and the landscape opened up, wide and barren and bleak in congruence with her own inner landscape. She walked and walked to where the rocky ground began to give way to endless expanses of sand and dust and sun.

Away from the town, it seemed safe to stop, and tiredness overtook her. The girl sat down beside a rocky outcrop, leaning against its shady sides. Held by the rocks and the Earth, she opened her heart to the great Mother below and out into her arms she poured her tears, her pain, her desolation, her emptiness. Heron was left feeling spent, drained and devoid of hope and with no care for her fate. A light had been extinguished. And without it, she felt diminished, reduced. Everything seemed futile and pointless.

A warm breeze started to rise. It stroked her tired body, ran its fingers through her hair and wiped her tears. As it caressed her, she sank into its warm undulating waves and drifted into sleep. The breeze continued to cleanse the debris of her experience; the spirits of the air stroking her brow and smoothing her nerves.

She slept a dull and deadened sleep, just the ravens walking over her body. She felt their claws pressing on her skin, the weight of the birds. And she did not care. Peck, peck, peck. She felt nothing.

Heron woke with a start and sat up, scrabbling back close against the rocks. Disoriented and alarmed, she tried to take in the sight before her. A man, some boys and many straggling sheep. The man looked at her. His eyes were gentle and full of concern. He wore a long and tattered robe with a rope tied around it. He carried a long staff and his face bore the weathering of many seasons spent out in the elements; many deep lines carved from a lifetime squinting against the sun and wind. She felt he was some kind of nomad. Him, the boys, the sheep all passing by.

The boys gathered behind the man a respectful distance away. He was their father. The boys, too, looked like they were part of the land, sculpted by it, connected to it. And the sheep bleated their reverberating cries. Heron wondered what they were saying. A simple sound. Others responded with their warbling voices. The constant sound of bleating back and forth became a reassuring background mesh of resonance against which the scene unfolded.

The man spoke to her. An enquiry, his eyes concerned at her predicament, at her aloneness in the scrubland. Heron's eyes held onto his enquiring gaze, but the answer was too enormous for her to convey.

He reached out a hand and beckoned her to stand. Her shoulders suddenly folded forwards and her body involuntarily collapsed in helplessness and tears pricked her eyes. Perplexed by his discovery, the man scooped her up and held her in his arms like a lamb. The boys followed their father as they strode forward. And the sheep bleated. Heron held onto their constant sound and closed her eyes as she was carried, limbs swinging limp and empty in the bewildered man's arms.

21

ary Magdalene was not a whore. She was none of the things that were subsequently written about her to discredit the role of the sacred feminine in the story of Christ. She was raped in retrospect by the powers that be.

But the eternal truth can never be destroyed. Only its expression. The expression of the full Christed feminine was persecuted for millennia. All of her mystical facets, her womanly powers, her knowing, her womanly wisdom, were annihilated dare they show their forms. Women were tortured, burned and killed.

They were told: Come to the men only with your succour. Come only with your nurturing and caring for the vulnerable. Be exalted only for your compassion and your selflessness. You will thrive as a half-woman. You will live, be granted an existence by the powers that be if you make this half your whole. Live in denial of your full power and in time you will forget the depths of your womanhood, the power of your womb, your unstoppable creative power, your deep dark beauty within.

But it will simmer, thick and still as a waiting womb, waiting to return and share her bounty, her magic, her salvation.

And now, times are different. The rapist has gone, been expunged, extracted; the last of his fibres tweezed from Mary

Magdalene. And here she stands. I am the Magdalene. The divine feminine and Heron is the wound. A muted, ravaged force who knew the Light of Christ because she was the Light of Christ.

Listen to the woman, the wise woman, the crone. Her eyes see with the eyes of Mother Earth. They see the destruction of the mother planet with the wisdom born of the remembrance of the destruction of her own feminine creative potential.

Her eyes ache. For too long they have looked upon the masculine domination, the mindless rape of the great woman, Mother Earth.

And the Great Mother rises; like the Magdalene, she is whole. She comes back into parity with the masculine to take her place side by side in the harmony of the universe. Feminine and masculine in balance.

Listen to Mother Earth and act accordingly, and she will create for you the heaven on Earth for which you yearn.

Listen. Listen! She is calling.

'Stop raping me, start serving me. And I will give you bounty beyond your wildest dreams. I warn you that this is imperative. I give you this to help you understand the way things work. It is not personal, it just is. You make a choice and there is an outcome. I urge you to make a different choice. A respect for the feminine. Women, respect yourselves; men, respect your women; and all lay yourselves at the feet of the great Mother, the Earth. For you are all her children. And in your humility, you will inherit the bounty of the Earth. Continue with your hubris and ideas of superiority and you will inherit the bleak, ravaged and desolate remnants of your Great Mother. Limp and empty like a lamb in the arms of a bewildered man.'

22

Mariam was gripped with panic. She searched frantically throughout the dwelling house. She knew the girl was gone. Her heart was tearing, cleaving with each empty room she overturned. There was nothing as she searched outside. Her face was taut with alarm, dread and a hideous realisation that Heron had been taken. Mariam felt the loss as if it were her own child and now Heron's disappearance blew open the pain that she felt at the separation from her own daughters. With stark and brutal ruthlessness, her hidden pain of foregoing her own children, abandoning them, was thrust into her awareness. Her guilt chided her; she doubted herself, her reckless abandonment of children. Her inattention, her lapse of judgement had left the girl in peril. She knew deep within her that this was serious; something unknown but very bad and sinister had happened.

Mariam tried to keep the waves of dread from consuming her. Heron was obedient; she would never have left the room. She had been taken, of that Mariam was sure. Guilt tightened its grip. She had neglected the girl, been so preoccupied with the threats to Yeshua that were in the ether that she took her attention off the child of Light. Her mind was scattered. She couldn't allow herself to feel the full depths of the dread she sensed. The predators circling around Yeshua had picked off the easy prey. The low-hanging fruit.

Her heart thumped in her chest. She was immobilised by her fear. Yeshua stood in front of her and held up his palms. He held her swirling terror and fragmented thoughts in the space between them. She breathed as he held it all and the tears began to fall. He kept a field of safety around her as she allowed the torment to pass through until some coherence returned.

Yeshua comforted her, "I have spoken to the men and sent them forth. They have relatives and connections in these parts." His words encouraged her. Yeshua's calmness pervaded and she leaned into and borrowed his faith until hers could be restored.

The shepherd had carried the girl for some time, but his arms did not ache. Followed by the boys and the sheep, they walked into the town. The shepherd took the girl to the large watering well. He knew it would be buzzing with chattering women. And so it was; the meeting place where mothers and children gathered, laughing, gossiping and scolding. The women fell into silence as the man approached and stood before them. A woman leapt up as she saw Heron laying limply in his arms. Quickly, she cupped water from a vessel and traced it over her face. She ran her wet hands over the child's parched lips, parting them and cupping water into her mouth. She was overcome with a powerful mothering instinct to revive the child.

Mariam's heart ached. This beautiful child with her special gifts; an innocent, open to the heavens above and the great Mother beneath. As if she were hardly here as she spanned the invisible forces of the two. An ethereal child, burgeoning with possibility, light of body and at one with the creative forces of the universe. A precious ghost of a child. And now, at the mercy of a harsh and violent world, like a lamb to the slaughter. A sweet lamb with few outer resources to survive on her own without protection. It was too painful to contemplate.

Mariam sat in desperation and reached up through the crystalline grid of everything in search of answers. She laid her heart bare, opening, surrendering to some greater power, to the great universal mystery, and she let her question go into the hands of divine grace.

The other women at the well crowded around, lifting Heron proprietorially from the shepherd's arms and asking questions of the man, who had no answers. Heron was too exhausted to react. She lay propped in a woman's lap as she knelt, cradling her on the ground. Heron heard the women shouting instructions across the market. Soon, she felt honey on her lips and a boy came running with fresh bread from the market stove, and her body began to recharge with the sustenance and the care of the women. The girl would tell them nothing. It was a mystery. No name, no home, no mother. The word spread quickly; the story of the girl found in the desert was making its way through the grapevine, the chattering network of gossiping people.

Mariam was alert, she could feel it coming. She could feel the network of chatter in the ether.

One of Yeshua's men walked through the market. He was asking questions and putting out the word of the lost girl among his connections in the town. This became a second chattering network of gossiping people. The network of searching energy had its partner; the network of energy that was, in return, looking for it.

The two attracting fields of gossip were on trajectories that would converge. Mariam focused on their intersection. Her intuition took her towards the town. She was carried by unseen forces and instinctively followed to where the tapestry was at its thickest among the chattering women at the well. The thread was alive and growing in her heart and Mariam started to run.

78

She dodged the dawdling townsfolk; their inertia irritating her as her own urgency intensified.

And there was Heron. Mariam gave a silent glance upwards in thankful prayer. And she descended on the child. "My child!" she cried. And as a lioness roared inside her, she plucked Heron from the woman's lap and lifted her. Mariam clung to the girl, clutched her head close to her shoulder like an infant and together they wept. Tears fell as the tension turned to relief and then to a deep-bonded comfort. And their hearts gradually synchronised and beat in time together.

Mariam scanned the women at the well and nodded her tearful gratitude to them. No one spoke as Mariam carried the girl away. They watched as the child slid to the ground onto her feet and walked beside the woman. The woman held her hand tightly. This time, it was Mariam who didn't want to let go.

Something in what happened that day bound them. She knew they were forever connected by these events. It was sealed like a bonding waxed seal, stamped on their hearts, connecting them through eternity.

23

Together, they returned to the dwelling house. Heron stayed inside. The woman of the house had been charged with sitting with her. Her small offerings of conversation went unanswered and so they fell into silence and the woman occupied herself twirling a spindle, spinning fleece into strands of yarn. Rhythmically, she spun out the fibres and hummed quietly to herself. It was a mutually acceptable and kindly arrangement. The woman was simple and loving, and it reminded Heron of her own mother's care.

Heron didn't feel the loss of her mother, another thought too painful to indulge, so – together with the rape – she kept it on the other side of her numbness. And she reinforced the layers in between to deaden herself and distance herself from her difficult and unwelcomed feelings, which threatened to break through into her awareness from time to time.

Later, as dusk was falling, some sort of disturbance was growing outside. Yeshua and the men were being besieged by the townspeople, as if something calamitous was driving them to the man they now looked to for their answers.

Heron moved over to the window. She placed her fingers on the ledge of the window opening and leaned forward just enough so that she could see the small crowd gathered outside. Yeshua held his palms up and spoke to the people. They were agitated; some unrest, some instability, some upheaval was threatening.

She watched the Light of Yeshua and the darkness the people spoke of, which they brought to him in their concerns. Any level of horror from man to man now seemed possible and real after what she had endured at the hands of the Roman.

The darkness that the people brought with them felt wholly congruent to the girl. The darkness of which they spoke had the same flavour as the darkness she could still taste, the darkness she had absorbed from the Roman.

Heron's mind raced to quell her rising panic. She pulled back from the window opening and began to walk back and forth, her pacing fuelled by her unexpressed emotion. She descended into inner turmoil. She tried to suppress the horror of the brutal man the day before and tried to make sense of the matching darkness that was approaching Yeshua. The girl paced and plucked at her tunic, fighting her own system's desire to release these feelings in tears. She held them in. She feared she would be overwhelmed and swept away if she gave them space and allowed the enormity of it to flow through her into the great grids. And so, she paced and wrung her fingers and breathed great anxious sighs. And the woman spun her yarn and watched on, pained at what she saw, but unable to help the girl.

Mariam burst into the room. "Yeshua is leaving tonight. It is not safe for him here." She registered the alarm in Heron's face. "Don't worry, child, all will be well," she added with a strained smile and touched her shoulder gently in an attempt to reassure her. But her words did little to assuage the girl's mounting anxiety.

Heron's world was now a confused tangle of fear. Bad things were happening and it was getting worse. Life was not safe anymore. The tiny strands of unease that were in the air as she and Mariam left Yeshua in the desert a few weeks before had burgeoned and amplified. The menace had mushroomed out of all proportion and was now dominating the landscape. It obliterated the days of Light and love and magic that had drawn her on this journey with these people, and nourished her heart with its truth and mystical possibility.

That part of her was now barely reachable. The threats in this earthly world, the material violence, the bodily damage overshadowed her knowledge of a higher, finer way of being.

She clung to Mariam and Mariam held her close. Mariam knew the trauma Heron had endured. She had seen the blood and the theft of the Light in her eyes. "We will follow when it is safe, but, for now, Yeshua must go."

It was strangely quiet later. Yeshua and the men had gone quickly, leaving an eerie vacuum. In the darkness, Mariam lay next to the girl on the mattress on the floor. Heron held onto the arms that encircled her and she curled up like a foetus. Mariam curled herself around the child, comforted by her warmth. Mariam felt something in the girl let go and surrender into her embrace and Mariam caught her. Her heart became the enormous canyon, the unbreakable eternal vastness. And Mariam's body surrounded the foetus as it sobbed. Mariam allowed herself to merge with the child and absorbed her into the depths of her womb to keep her safe forever.

24

Yeshua looked into the distance; he knew Mariam and the girl would be arriving soon – that they were following. He looked to the East. He knew his time on Earth was nearing its end. He knew that soon he would die. He was reconciled with this. Some greater part of him knew the order of things, the divine perfection in the order of events. Yet he looked out to the horizon across the desert. He wanted Mariam with him. He needed his beloved in that moment, his reflection, his tower, the one who would understand.

Behind him were his companions. A canopy hung out from a low dwelling. The men stood beneath it, ruminating, discussing strategy, looking for solutions. Yeshua wanted to be on his own, away from their futile deliberations, and he stood, looking out and waiting. He needed Mariam before he could go any further.

The mood was sombre. Mariam silently stared ahead as her camel lurched its way across the sands. Heron's animal followed, laden with goods. The girl was in a dense and soporific daze, her sensitivities now unavailable. The sky became black and clear and the firmament looked down on them; their twinkling blanket of stars was no solace to the travellers.

Yeshua spotted them approaching, a moving shadow against the night sky. A dance of delight and anguish played in his heart.

They came closer. Mariam was on the left and the girl on the right. He saw them as one. He knew the child had become an inseparable part of Mariam. He could see how she was held safely in Mariam's energy field and Mariam would not be parted from her. Something had happened and where they had been two, they were now one.

His eternal heart was activated. The part of him that he knew would live on and would continue for all time through the great grids once his body was no more. He became this part of himself and his heart intuitively connected to the invisible energies of the two approaching figures, transcending their earthly forms. He spontaneously stretched out his arms towards them.

To an onlooker, he was a man waiting to greet travellers in his arms, but his hands extended the distance between them across the sands and he cupped one in each hand. Mariam on his left hand, the girl on his right. He held their essences on his palms.

He pulled the essences of them to him and placed his hands over his heart. In that movement, he brought them with him, forever held, complete, together, eternal in the great connection with the All. The balance, the whole, would remain for eternity. It was the necessary balance, the sacred harmony between the masculine creative force and the feminine creative potential preserved through space and time.

He spun it into a helix, making a cord of the masculine and feminine energies, and threaded it into the heavens and threaded it into the core of the Earth. And it was sealed for all time in the consciousness of the universe.

And it would wait to be remembered, rediscovered, when the imbalance could no longer sustain. When the creaking and groaning of Mother Earth could bear the imbalance no longer. When her veins ran with poison, her resources were plundered and her pain too much to bear. And Mother would reactivate the sacred threads. She would uplift the women, call to them through their wombs to create change, to redress the balance, to heal and to activate the divine feminine within themselves. And to accept no less than the divine masculine in the balance with their men.

Mother Earth would recognise Heron, recognise the feminine wound, see herself in the girl, in all the girls, in all the women. All carrying the wounds from their connection to the lower aspects of the masculine. And to heal herself, she must heal Heron, heal the women, for they are all connected. It cannot be otherwise. To replenish her strength, to create her abundance, to nurture her children, Mother Earth must heal.

When Mother Earth looks at her daughters, at their dwindled and stifled creative power, she seeks to revive it as she revives her own. Their body is her body. She sends up her energies to raise the women, to heal them and bring back their mystical powers and their knowing from its exile.

It was Yeshua's understanding of this sacred law of the balance of the masculine and feminine that compelled him to preserve the template for eternity. His body would go and so would Mariam's, but the sacred blueprint of balance would survive. It comforted him; he did this for mankind. That they might remember and that, one day, it might actualise.

He watched Mariam getting closer. His appreciation of her opened him to the spaciousness of eternal love. He honoured her. She allowed him to fully embody his own divine state while she embodied her own. And the love was pure. He thought of his beloved wife, his equal, and how her life would be without him. He thought how they would still be together on different sides of the veil.

Yeshua knew that her future, her memory, her story, would always be connected to her relationship with him. She would not be seen objectively in her own right, in her own Light, he knew this. She would never be free from her entanglement with Yeshua and that incarnation. She was known; she was marked out and labelled. And so, he held her sacred essence entwined with his own, beyond the reach of the damnation that would follow her name.

And he held the girl. Mariam was protecting her preciousness. The child carried the pure and boundless creative potential of woman in her sovereignty. Mariam knew this was the true nature of the feminine and she would not let it go.

Yeshua saw that, unlike Mariam, the girl was unknown, unnoticed, a mute, a nobody, an everybody. So entwined with Mariam, Yeshua wove her into the crystal grid of everything for all time.

25

Heron brightened. She saw Yeshua in the distance and behind him a low building with a canopy held taught on upright poles, beneath which the men were talking. They were all standing up. Her heart lifted at the sight of Yeshua and she was suddenly excited to see him. She imagined the moment he would scoop her in his arms again and spin her to the ground as he had the last time they were reunited. She was ready to put her arms out to his.

The camels folded to their knees, but this time it was Mariam he was looking at as she climbed to the ground. Mariam walked slowly towards her husband. Heron watched their greeting. The merging of their eyes and their inner vision meeting, and she saw that much was conveyed without words and was understood between them.

Mariam turned to the girl. "You stay here for a moment," and she smiled an apology, knowing the girl had wanted to greet Yeshua. Obediently, Heron stayed, elevated on the camel's back, and she watched as Yeshua and Mariam seemed to glide through the chattering men and disappeared through an opening into a space beyond.

Patiently, she waited. Now that they had stopped moving, she could smell the pungent aroma of the camel as it rose off its warm body. Earthy, thick and comforting. A warm reliable animal. Inwardly, she thanked the beast for its service, its dependability, for carrying her safely.

She turned her attention to the scene in front of her. Torches were placed in the ground, which illuminated the canopy. The men were familiar to her. She had observed them by the fire and in the dwelling house. They seemed to travel everywhere with Yeshua. They didn't speak to her, they never bothered with her and she thought of them as Yeshua's business.

She felt their differing energies; a varied mix of men, their different characters. They clustered in small groups of twos and threes, each group held together by the common vibration of the men of whom it comprised. One group was vibrating with concern, a profound sense of worry, and although she was too far away to hear their words, she knew they spoke of hope, of rescue, of plans to solve the problem. They were earnest and honourable in their thinking.

Two other men were at a loss. They had come to the end of their ideas, drawn together in a mutual air of helplessness. A loyalty, a fraternity hung in the air, but they were at a loss, hopeless as to what actions they might take.

To the right was another group of three. They felt different. She sensed that they knew they were threaded into the impending catastrophe surrounding Yeshua. One man was whispering urgently to the other two, who listened to his concerns. Heron could feel his fear mounting. Fear that by being close to Yeshua, he was implicated, connected. The more focus this man put on his own perceived peril, the greater his separation became from Yeshua, his loyalty to him abandoned. He spoke in hushed tones and from a fearful place, his own inner vulnerability pulling at him. And Heron knew what a man was capable of when his vulnerabilities rose up. A man could stop at nothing to quell the voice of his own inner fears.

She focused in on the whispering man and her heart raced. This was not good; this was really not good for Yeshua. Her panic rose.

At that moment, Yeshua emerged through the opening and, to Heron's consternation, he called to the whisperer. Her heart leapt. The whispering man turned and faced Yeshua with a change of energy, an agreeable smile to disguise his growing and fearful agenda of self-preservation. Heron gasped as she watched on. Her throat tightened; she wanted to scream to Yeshua, "Look out! There is danger! Don't trust him!" but nothing came out, the words shrivelled and entangled in her throat. She sat in panic as the man disappeared through the opening with Yeshua. But Yeshua knew the man's heart. He knew his disposition; he knew he was the one who would take on the task, who would be tempted by the money, by the deal – the one for whom Yeshua's Light had a price.

The torches flickered and she waited for what seemed a very long time. She breathed in the camel, its bulk beneath her like ballast that anchored her. She placed her hand over her heart and steadied herself.

From the canopy, Mariam strode towards her. She smiled and reached up to the girl and lifted her down in her arms. "Let's eat," she said lightly and they walked together, hand in hand, and joined the men who were sitting inside, eating from bowls.

Heron nursed her bowl. From the periphery, she watched the adults. Mariam was sitting beside Yeshua. Heron saw them as an equilateral triangle. One unit made up of two back-to-back mirrored right-angled triangles. The upper point seemed to extend forever into the grids of the heavens and their shared base was wide and stable in the Earth, a part of her matrix.

Others had energy flying off them in strands of worry, and the whispering man was heavy and silent and seemed preoccupied as he pushed his food around his bowl. Something in him had separated off and his thoughts were now for himself. Outwardly, he looked normal, but with her inner vision she could see he was hardening into a kernel of self-serving, of self-preservation. His ties with the group were atrophying.

The whisperer spotted Heron watching him. She knew something. He suspected she somehow saw the truth: his abandonment of the group's cause and his creeping adoption of his own separate, individual cause. His thoughts of betrayal.

Their eyes met. He stood up and picked his way around the edge of the group to where Heron sat. Nobody noticed as he smiled and offered his hand. He ushered her through to a side room. "You'll be much more comfortable here," he said. He had never heard the girl speak but he wanted her gone, urgently. She knew something. He smiled sweetly at her and repeated his assertion that she would prefer it here. His eyebrows raised as he looked pointedly at her, making it clear that his suggestion was not up for debate. She would be staying here.

He looked questioningly at the girl. Who was she, anyway? And what was she doing here? Why was she so special to Mariam and Yeshua? Heron sensed he would not harm her. He knew she was precious to Mariam and Yeshua and it would be sensible to look as though he valued her, too. It would do him and his agenda no favours to appear harsh to the girl, so he smiled and brought her more food and water.

He was threatened by her knowing, but with his smiling and apparent concern, he gave the impression of being caring should anyone be looking on. But Heron knew she was being intimidated, silenced, shut down, excluded.

He returned to the group of adults, free from the girl's gaze. He had removed the niggling thorn from his side.

26

Presently, Mariam came to find her. There was relief on her face and she puffed out a long sigh and smiled. "Are you alright?" she enquired gently. Heron nodded.

Mariam brought her things for the night. She rolled out a mattress and carried in some blankets. She settled the girl. Heron was glad to lay down. Glad to rest her weary body and to close her tired eyes. Mariam pulled the blanket up to Heron's shoulders and stroked her arms from above the blanket. She cupped the girl's head and stroked her hair. There didn't seem to be anything to say.

Heron heard Mariam leave and she opened her eyes. Her body was drained and ready to sleep, but some inner flywheel continued to spin and didn't allow her mind to rest. She listened to the distant sounds of the adults and she must have drifted off eventually for she was suddenly startled awake again and now it was completely dark. Everything was silent, but her other senses were engulfed. She caught her breath and her eyes became wide. A distinctive pungent smell was creeping through the air. She recognised it immediately as the vapours of the spikenard oil. It drifted into her room and she sensed the beautiful woman of the nard who showed the dying the glory of the paradise that awaits.

Her mind raced. Who was dying? The nard was beautiful and sensed her fears. It wrapped around her. The particles touched her senses and Heron began to cry. She didn't know why the nard was here; she didn't understand. But the nard didn't make mistakes, she was here for a reason. Heron cried until all her tears were spent. Her exhaustion was complete and she fell into the embrace of the spirit of the oil and sleep overtook her.

Mariam woke her as the sun rose. The girl had slept and slept. Mariam's hand stroked her cheek and her gentle words roused the girl. Heron enjoyed Mariam's touch on her face; she luxuriated in the love brushing her cheeks and she gradually opened her eyes. Mariam's fingers were heavy with the smell of the nard. Heron's awakening in the night flooded back to her with alarm and she remembered her encounter with the spirit of the spikenard oil.

"Heron, my love, this is hard for me to say, but you must stay here now. I have instructed the woman of this place to care for you. I know it is frightening and you have been through so much, but I am asking you to trust that this is for the best. She will look after you and provide food and shelter here and she will make sure you come to no harm. You will be safe."

The aroma of the spikenard was powerful. The oil was staining Mariam's robe, too. With her eyes, Heron traced the spots one to the next on the fabric across Mariam's knees as she knelt beside her. It was an ominous dot to dot. Heron heard the instructions she had been given, but was fixed with alarm on the oil stains on Mariam's robe, still pumping out their familiar vibration. What had Mariam been doing with the nard last night?

And with that, Mariam left her. Heron felt numb and lost, but clung bravely to her obedience and trust. It was all she had. The place was already silent; everyone else had left.

The woman of the house was amenable and kept the girl occupied with chores, which Heron willingly undertook. There were some chickens outside and Heron tended to them. They laid warm eggs, which she was tasked with collecting. She held each one carefully and she remembered holding the stoppered jar of spikenard with the same care in her cupped hands a few weeks ago when they had visited the dying woman. She held each egg like she had held the jar, close to her heart lest she drop it and loose the valuable contents.

How different it was now. The nard had filled the air at the old woman's bedside in the most loving caress, transcendent and blissful. And now the smell lingered in the dwelling and she couldn't bear to imagine why Mariam had administered it. To *whom* she had administered it. She closed down the thoughts and took the bowl of eggs she had collected and gave them to the woman. The woman took them with an approving smile and together they carried on with the chores. Heron swept the floors, removing the last traces of the adults and their activities from the night before. She moved absently with her long brush. She thought of Yeshua. She thought of the nard. But it was all too much; her heart was heavy and she lowered her gaze and lost herself in the rhythm of the brush. Swoosh, swoosh, its bristles flicked the dirt into an ever-increasing pile of dust and crumbs. She paused for a moment and slowly tidied the dust into a satisfyingly neat, regular-shaped pile, as if trying to herd her scattered feelings into some order, too.

She looked up again at the spot where Yeshua and Mariam had made an equilateral triangle in her inner vision the night before. In her mind's eye, she saw the triangle again. This time, it rotated through 180 degrees and a second identical triangle overlaid the first in perfect symmetry. It made a six-pointed star of two overlapping triangles. The triangles seemed to forge into one unbreakable symbol. Something of the balance of Mariam and Yeshua and their unbreakable union. She saw angels appear around it and her heart cracked. She was deeply touched by the symbolism, and tears rolled slowly and silently down her cheeks.

27

Something was in the air. Heron was outside again, tending the chickens. She enjoyed this daily job, but she paused and stood still and felt the atmosphere; something was brewing. As she contemplated this and tuned into the unwelcomed vibration, she found herself absently picking one grain at a time out of her hand and dropping it for the chickens. She was quite detached as she looked down and observed their frenzied jostling at her feet. They scrabbled and fought for the single grain as if they would never eat again. They flapped and crawled over each other to get to it. She dropped another grain into, what was now, a squawking frenzy. The once calm and harmonious flock was now suddenly in the grip of fear. Their fear of scarcity blinded them with some primitive survival instinct. Each single grain became the focus of the entire crowd. A dozen chickens descending on one small golden grain. And now they jostled and pecked at each other, and it was every man for himself. She felt the same vibration in the ether. It was all around the building in the air, too. Beyond the drama she had created with the chickens, another corresponding one was being created outside.

She came back from her reverie and saw the plight of the hungry chickens, the ruckus she had created by her actions, by her inattention. She quickly scattered great handfuls of golden grain across the ground. Appeased, the chickens quickly dispersed and scratched away in the dirt. The panic in the creatures was immediately forgotten. They were calm again. If only it were so easy to calm the drama with the people.

She imagined scattering golden grains over the greedy people to calm them and let them see that there is enough, that there's no need to fight. But she knew it would be futile, only holding back the inevitable. Once the grains were gone, they would be back to squabbling.

She saw the grain, the sacred golden seed in the heart of all beings. But mankind seemed blind to seeing his own. Incapable of recognising and nurturing his own golden grain within, his seed of divinity, his potential, his grace, his gifts, his highest nobility, his authentic power, his destiny. Like seeds, mankind's inner golden grain knows exactly what to do. It contains all the codes for the bountiful harvest it can become.

The golden grains in the people were unseen and she saw the scrabbling of mankind for power from outside of themselves, ignorant of their own unlimited supply of grain within. It was mankind's way of functioning, it seemed to the girl. Her heart ached. The air felt thick with it.

Heron had lived with Mariam and Yeshua, who knew about the sacred gold in the human heart. And they knew the girl saw it, too. They embodied and lived from their own inner grace. She now felt very alone and the gold became increasingly consumed by the darkness moving through the air.

She watched the comical, feathery creatures now happily going about their business. Bellies full of grain, a content and harmonious flock again, replete with gold. Man had an inner grain store in his heart, but just couldn't see it.

The air filled with sounds of people gathering and moving, of urgency. The woman came outside to find her. She was agitated and caught up in the fibres of the drama coming together in the air. "We must go. Quick, quick! Come on," she implored.

She and Heron joined the stream of people outside, who were all heading in the same direction. There was an excitement in the air, a common pull, a rising frenzy. Something was happening and it seemed to have an effect on all the townspeople, magnetising them to it. Heron let the woman pull her along, buffeted by the moving people and swept along by the current of the rising drama.

After a while, the woman suddenly pulled her to one side out of the fray and they stood still, waiting – it seemed – at this particular spot. She gripped tightly onto the girl's hand. The woman seemed to be looking for someone as she earnestly scanned the passing faces. Their spot was elevated and Heron watched the people pass by and funnel along into the road below.

It seemed to happen in the same instant. In the distance, among the crowds below, she saw Yeshua. She knew it was him. She only saw him from behind. His back was bare and on it he carried a long cross made of wood.

She reeled. She couldn't take in what she was seeing. There was Yeshua and there was the eye of the storm. A cyclone of people pulled into the unfolding events around him. Her pull to him was visceral, immediate. She focused in on Yeshua and he was surrounded by a pocket of high tension. The men around him, the ones in charge were like a tinderbox. Everything felt highly dangerous.

And in the same moment, Mariam appeared from the crowd and was by her side. She knelt and took both of Heron's hands in hers and their eyes met. No words were exchanged. They acknowledged the fear in each other's eyes. Heron pleaded with Mariam to take her with her. She wanted nothing more than to be with Mariam and go to Yeshua, to be with them where she belonged. Mariam read the girl, her plea, and for some moments she hesitated. Should she acquiesce and relieve the child of her pain? A part of her wanted the girl with her, too. Heron would not let go of her gaze. "Please," she implored.

Mariam's heart was breaking for the child. Her face tightened and tears brimmed in her eyes as she shook her head. She took the girl in her arms and her tears dropped on Heron's head. It was all too painful. She girded herself, loosened her hold and held Heron firmly by the shoulders at arm's length. "I'm sorry, it is no place for a child. You must stay here." And with that, she rose to her feet. She spoke briefly to the woman, who nodded her understanding that she must take the child back to safety. And without looking back, Mariam disappeared again into the current of moving people.

Heron's heart was cleaving. Mariam's rejection wounded her deeply. The noise of the crowd was increasing. People were shouting; a heady mix of fear and anticipation grew into a fervent unstoppable fever. She could barely put one foot in front of another. She knew her legs were there, dutifully keeping up with the woman as they waded against the tide, but she could hardly feel them. It was as if she was almost floating in the air, or at least some part of her was. A part that was taking refuge and being pulled along like a kite tethered to the woman by a thread.

The quiet of the dwelling house only amplified her sense of separation and inner cacophony. The turmoil, confusion and helplessness were overwhelming. Her stomach was shrunken to a tight kernel, hardened and clenched. Some part of her, in her despair, was opting out, leaving, and she sat like a shadow of herself. The woman was moving around, making heavy sighing sounds and busying herself, but her anxiety was palpable, too. Heron could not eat and neither could the woman. They poked their food around with no appetite.

The woman looped a skein of yarn around the girl's outstretched hands and she drew it from her and wound it into a neat ball. Heron took refuge in playing the child's part. She had done this many times with her mother. And she lost herself in the distant memory of a carefree childish world where bad things didn't happen and her mother would make everything alright. She fell into the soothing rhythm of the winding, lowering her wrists – left, right, left, right, left, right – to release the yarn to the woman. The yarn came to an end and dropped off Heron's hands. The ball was complete. It was done. The woman stood up and closed the shutters on the windows, sealing them in and the world out.

28

On that day, Mariam had knelt before Yeshua as he hung on the cross. She had willed her beloved across to the other side, to leave his body and join the source from whence he came. She held up her palms and held her heart wide open and activated the spirit of the spikenard. She had lifted him. His mother was there, too, and they both used the sacred oil, opening their hearts wide to Yeshua in the last service to their beloved. Tears poured as their hearts cracked. Cosmic light roared through them, breaking them wider and wider, and a portal opened. And in their devotion, their knowing of the eternity of life, and their love for Yeshua, they took away his suffering as he joined the continuum of Light.

Later, Mariam was alone with Yeshua's body; his empty, lifeless vessel laying on the stone floor. She knew that Heron must see him now. She knew the girl must feel the emptiness of his body. It was time. She sent word and Heron was brought to her by the woman.

Mariam was lost, deep in her silence, kneeling beside Yeshua's body. Everything was silent and still. The atmosphere was pure, calm, vacuous. Heron stared. The world stopped. Her eyes widened and she took in the sight of Yeshua's dead body on the floor. Silent, still, empty, vacant. Yeshua had gone. Mariam seemed elsewhere; she was unresponsive and Heron fell to her knees beside her. Her eyes fixed in horror on the blood-stained legs that lay in front of her. Lines of dried blood streaked down Yeshua's shins, crusting and matting into the hairs in curling black flakes like the cinders and ashes of his vital fluid.

Tears welled and her head spun. Some frantic part of her activated, desperate to do something. Her healing hands could help him maybe. She wanted to touch him. Instinctively, she reached out towards the bloodied leg stretched before her. With tears streaming down her face and her hands quivering, her little palms reached out. She needed to touch him.

Mariam was kneeling to her right and in her trance-like state she reached across and gently lowered Heron's hands. "No," she said. "It's too late." Her face was hollow and ghostly as she kept Heron's hands held firmly down.

Heron looked across in disbelief; she couldn't understand why Mariam had done this. Why she had quelled her instinct, her desire, her need. It wounded her deeply. Every fibre of her wanted to touch Yeshua. Inwardly, she riled against Mariam. In her childlike confusion, her heart broke at Mariam's actions and the sight of Yeshua's empty body before her.

She was angry at Mariam, angry at the theft of Yeshua's life, his Light, his power. Anger and blame overtook her, reverberating through her entire body. She was incensed as she felt the vibration of man taking another's power. The injustice. It ignited her rage at the man who had brutally raped her and taken her own Light. It felt the same to her; a congruent energy. And in her mind, she looked over her shoulder to where she felt the Roman was looking on at his murderous work. She knew that this was his doing, too, and she seethed, "You did this!"

She sobbed uncontrollably. Her body swayed and rocked. Grief crashed over her in tidal waves, spiked with anger and futility and the whole landscape in between from volcanic rage to desolate barren darkness. Mariam was silent, seemingly uncaring, almost as if she were elsewhere. She offered no comfort. Heron hated Mariam; she blamed her for her pain. She hated the Roman for what he had done to her and what he had done to Yeshua, but it was somehow safer to hate Mariam.

She just wanted to touch Yeshua, that's all she wanted. To touch his flesh. It was an overwhelming urge to somehow honour him with her touch, place herself at his feet, offer a gold coin at the portal of his Light. To honour the commitment she had made to him in the cave. Let him know she would never forget. Let him know he was forever in her heart. A touch would do all that and she needed to do it, and Mariam had put her hands down, restrained her. Mariam denied her what her very essence yearned to do, needed to do. Something was incomplete. She would always want that touch. It was agony. Her pain at Yeshua's death and Mariam's heartless actions was unbearable. Her silent rage swirled and spiralled inside her like a rising fiery serpent, which coiled tightly around her muted throat and sealed her pain there forever.

Heron snatched her hands away from Mariam's grasp. Mariam didn't stop her as she stood up and stormed away.

Why had Mariam not let her touch him?! She and Yeshua had started their journey with a bonded holding of hands and she desperately needed to bow to that. It had to be. Some part of her knew she would always be seeking that touch. It was etched into her in that moment. Mariam's actions had sealed her desire to honour Yeshua and deep down she knew she would seek him out through all the grids, through time and space. The pain would keep her searching and searching for Yeshua and that one touch would complete their contract, discharge their obligation, settle the bond that was made in the cave.

After Heron left, Mariam lay down beside her beloved. She lay her body next to his and her heart broke. Her job was done. She did it for Yeshua. She did it for Heron. She did it for mankind. She knew the essence of the girl would keep searching. By lowering her hands and stopping their union, she stopped the completion of their business. She held back time. She held back time until it was safe. She protected their holy contract, kept it in abeyance until a time when Heron could touch Yeshua again. At a time when the sacred balance of creation between the masculine and the feminine could be restored. When it could be reignited in the consciousness of mankind, as a guiding light, a torch, a way finder for humanity.

Mariam's guidance had directed her. She was guided to do this by some higher part of herself, some part that knew the bigger picture beyond that which she could see, but which she trusted. And so, it was left like this for Heron. A rift with Mariam and unfinished business with Yeshua. A fracture, a wound waiting to be healed.

29

The girl didn't see it, but she had been given a gift. Her essence, her soul, would carry the unfinished business from that incarnation, from those events, from the broken connection to Yeshua and the rift with Mariam. And the potential would always be there for the completion, the reconnection, the settlement, the healing of those wounds. The coming together in some other place and time.

Mariam had been the caretaker of Heron. The girl was the possibility, the potential, the nobody, the everybody, and Mariam was heavy with guilt that she had failed to protect her pure crystalline nature. It was like a millstone around her neck, threaded through her consciousness. The weight of the male abuse hung between them – the desire of a man to dominate and not revere the female form. In her own experience, Mariam had only known the sacred reverence of Yeshua. Her body held the imprint of the sacred reverence of a man, and yet its opposite resided close by with her connection to Heron. Mariam and Heron were interwoven. Their love and their rupture connected them.

Mariam's influence, her consciousness, would continue to guide Heron through all her incarnations as she had in their life together. Mariam would whisper into her heart through time and space and guide her back to Yeshua. And by the girl touching Yeshua again, by Mariam guiding her there, she herself would be healed. Mariam's pain would transform.

And the time came two thousand years later when a woman became the searching incarnation. She relentlessly sought the Light of Yeshua in her life. Her quest was to purify her own heart, to heal her own wounds, to refine her own golden grain, to uncover her destiny within it. Gradually, her heart opened until its vibration resonated with that of the essence of Heron. And in her visions, through time and space, through the great grids of everything, she found the mute girl. And she found Yeshua. She bowed before Yeshua and tears pricked from gratitude to him for keeping Heron's essence safe. It was time for Yeshua to release her, to allow her crystalline template to be returned to the body of a woman in whom Heron was now safe and to where she was needed. And with the touch, the reunion, he released her, he returned her, he gave her back to the woman who had been searching.

And Heron understood why Mariam did what she did, why she prevented her completion with Yeshua, why she held back their union until this time. And in Heron's realisation, the girl bowed in gratitude and wept with forgiveness at the feet of her beloved Mariam and their rift was transformed. Mariam was released. In holding down Heron's hands, she knew she was delaying her own release, her own return. And the divine feminine in all seekers would respond to the waves of her unconditional love of all humanity.

And as the consciousness of Mary Magdalene lit ever brighter inside the seeking woman, the moon supported her and Mother Earth roared through her as an embodied physical expression of the divine feminine.

And Mother Earth smiled at all her beautiful children. And Mother Earth wept at the perfection of it all.

The divine feminine aspect is returning in all seekers at this time. Wounds are being healed to evolve the hearts of humanity at a time in the journey of mankind when the balance of the divine feminine is needed. When the forests burn and the oceans choke and Mother Earth is fighting for her life.

Like Mariam at the side of Yeshua's body, Mother Earth also has to be the wise and brave mother, seeing the bigger picture that her children cannot see. From her maternal wisdom, she must hurt the beloved children of her planet to preserve the creative potential, the balance. And like Heron, mankind does not understand their wise mother's actions.

The children of Mother Earth will rile against her, try to control her. And Mother Earth's heart breaks at causing suffering to her children, just as Mariam's heart broke at causing suffering to Heron. But it must be done. For the greater good. To preserve the potential, to keep the highest creative possibility alive.

To give humankind the chance to uncover its divinity, to balance its masculine and feminine aspects, and to choose to create from there. From its balanced heart and mind, from its golden grain. From love. And when mankind discovers his inner riches, he will no longer seek with greed and fear the satisfaction he craves from outside of himself with the destruction that brings. He will see that the satisfaction he is seeking is inside himself. Inner harmony will create outer harmony. And Mother Earth will smile.

As Heron is found and her wounds from that time are healed, the fiery serpent around her neck, her pain and rage from Yeshua's death and Mariam's actions, loosens and disintegrates. Her throat shines white and pure and becomes part of her divine crystalline template. Her inner wisdom and her pure heart can join together and funnel her heart-wisdom unhindered through her communication centre. Her vocal cords stretch and saturate with Light. Heron's voice unfolds and comes to life. Like the tightly packed bud of a rose erupts into a cloud of petals, Heron's voice bursts into its full potential, her muteness healed.

And the words spill from her mouth, they pour forth, great waves of the unspoken within her. The words pour until her essence has wrung them all out. The last unspoken drips of that incarnation fall onto this page until her story is told.

30

Mariam left on a boat and sailed for many days. But she could not leave behind the thought of the girl. Yeshua was gone and she had had to let go of the girl. She had asked that angels take the girl safely back home to her mother. And an archangel in the form of a man, a tall man in coarse brown robes, had walked by Heron's side and guided her back to her mother. And there they were. Mariam and Heron, the wound strung between them like a gaping tear in the tapestry. Both with heavy hearts. Both alone. Both burdened with the pain of the events that bound them.

And the hole in the tapestry was like a portal through all time and space. The collective wounds of the feminine creating a cavernous hole of pain in the tapestry of life.

But the hole in the tapestry is being rewoven. The threads are stretching from one side to another. Today, women are reweaving the broken threads as they heal their wounds of oppression and persecution by the masculine. Each time a woman heals, each time she heals her ancestors, a thread is stretched across the hole, providing a warp for the next weft, and woman by woman, the hole is spanned with new threads of the sacred feminine. Until the repair is complete. Until the threads are strongly in place and the tapestry is whole again.

As the wound of Mary Magdalene, the wound of the sacred feminine in all beings is healed, her consciousness strengthens and evolves. The Light of the sacred feminine floods the consciousness of humanity like a golden elixir to soothe, uplift and empower the recovery of the feminine aspect and restore balance.

31

Heron never saw Mariam again. She fled into the desert, despairing and desolate. She was intercepted by the man, the archangel, whom Mariam had sent. He had suddenly appeared by her side and, in desperation, she looked into his eyes. She saw a sanctuary, a refuge; she knew she was safe. His gentle tone unravelled her and she grabbed onto him and buried her face in the coarse weave of his robes and sobbed helplessly. She began to twist with pain inside and she gripped and twisted her fingers in the fabric and she howled like a wounded animal and she pummelled and punched her small fists into the man's body. The man allowed himself to be what she needed. To contain her, to swallow her pain, to absorb it. It pained him, but he did it for her, for his brothers' deeds, for the wrongs of man. He would not let her down.

They travelled together in easy silence. They were unlikely but harmonious companions, and the man took her back to her mother. He felt the girl's excitement rising as the spool of thread between her and her mother was reeling in, spinning faster, bringing Heron home. And he stood still with his arms by his sides and watched from a distance as Heron, without looking back, ran into her mother's arms. He felt a strange pang in his heart that she had just taken off without acknowledging him, without saying goodbye; he felt strangely forgotten. Though he knew she owed him nothing, he felt inexplicably sad. He watched their reunion, their joy, and he turned and left and suddenly felt lonelier than ever.

Heron's life was blighted and blessed all at once and her story remained untold. She grew into the wordless woman who walked through the same marketplace she had as a child. She became known as a healer in her town. Her husband led her through the crowds, clearing a path, protecting her and setting up the small wooden bench on which she sat. People came great distances. Snaking lines of people waited their turn. Heron looked into their eyes and laid her hands upon them. She did her best with her gifts.

But her heart was always heavy. A shadow cast over her golden grain. Her husband was loyal, protective and devoted. A woman needed a man and she was lucky. They had no children. And so, this was her life for many years.

Her husband was at her side as her body faded. He cared tenderly for her and rarely left her side. His distress and pain at her dying was a burden for Heron. She was happy to go. She had always felt guilty that she hadn't been able to return the depth of his devotion. It had become too far out of balance now. For she had known Yeshua and the fullness of her devotion still dwelt with him. How could she convey that to this good man? She was happy to go, ready to go and leave her body and her guilt behind. She slipped across the veil and her heart reached out into the eternal field and she laid herself bare, giving herself up into the arms of angels. And there she lay, bathed and held in their light. And she was spun in a gossamer web of the finest and brightest light, like a field pulsing her highest signature. And she waited to be reclaimed, remembered, recognised. Wrapped in her gossamer blanket, she was connected to each of her incarnations, that they might refine themselves to ever higher vibrations of love and compassion, getting closer and closer to the gossamer parcel of Heron's essence.

Part Two

ASAPH

32

The boy walked away. He wasn't sure what had happened, but he felt he had been touched or seen in the most beautiful way. It had affected him profoundly. He had been angry at the oil merchant at the market and he had fought in the dust with the other boy. The boy who was smiling, always smiling; he had wanted to smash that smile off his face. He had been victorious and something had made him walk over to the strange girl who stood alone watching the fight. To the girl who didn't speak; the one who didn't join in. To the girl who looked into his eyes.

Whatever the girl had, he wanted that. He was magnetised, impressed and his thoughts were flooded with the feeling of her gaze. She had something he longed for, something intangible. It was unnerving but at the same time compelling, as if some truth in him had been touched by some truth in her.

He carried on walking after he left the girl. He felt light. He felt as though she held an answer. Her look made him feel safe and held and, at the same time, magnificent. The magnificence of his own truth. He felt a desire to bow down before her. He wanted to give himself to the girl, to what came through her. Some ultimate feminine expression of love, of understanding, of holding, of non-judgment, of grace. Something of beauty – a pure beauty that felt sublime to him.

He let the feelings wash through his body at first like a salve, soothing and smoothing him, and then invigorating and exhilarating him. He filled up with his own inner beauty, his desire to honour her. His desire to lay himself at the feet of whatever she was. It swam through him, imprinting in him a knowing of her, of her sacred nature. It embedded deep into a masculine part of himself. It awoke and invited that sacred aspect of himself into being. Somehow, in their exchange, she had opened up a part of him that could never be closed and it was intoxicating – his own sacred masculine aspect. It was illuminating him with each step until he felt as though a golden star was bursting in his heart.

He kept walking; he kept swimming in glorious golden starlight. It was as if she had ignited him, switched on a light in him that he knew would burn forever. It was a light that could not be extinguished.

By the time he neared his destination, his heart was expanded with the golden light. He wasn't ready or able to encounter anybody yet; he felt too strange and so he lowered himself to the ground and sat alone under a tree. What was happening to him? This blinding, dazzling starlight seemed to take over the whole of him. He was barely there. He must be invisible, he thought. He felt invisible. As if he had no body. He felt as if he had become the starlight.

What was this? He could make no sense of it. It felt as if the Gods in the heavens were striking a starburst through his heart.

Gradually, the light began to ease and he felt his body thrum with its vibration. His breathing, which seemed to have been suspended, returned. He sat with his eyes closed as his whole system gently reverberated. The alarm he felt was amplified by the awe at the enormity of the experience. Gradually, his racing heart began to regulate, and in the stillness that followed, on the blank canvas of his closed eyes, an angel appeared before him.

It had huge wings, which seemed to expand and extend wide enough to encompass both him and the whole of the tree against which he sat. The wings stretched and encircled them both. The boy and the tree. It made a seal. The wings sealed the boy and the tree together in a scintillating ring of light.

The boy felt the angel convey to him, "You are bonded forever with the tree." That was its message. "You, the tree, together" and some kind of ring – a hoop of light around him and the tree, bound together by the angel.

The boy opened his eyes. His mind scrabbled to make sense of the experience. No one passing by seemed to have noticed anything untoward. He breathed deeply and tried to calm himself. He felt the tree supporting his back and looked up at its thin branches arching over him. He had never paid much attention to trees before. They were unremarkable, familiar, inanimate; they were functional, they provided fruit, they provided shade. They held no interest. He'd barely noticed them. And yet, suddenly, it was as if this tree was smiling at him. They had shared the experience it seemed; they had been joined together somehow by it, like partners. The tree seemed to be alive, as though part of it had some living, almost human aspect that could communicate with him.

He sat there, trying desperately to make sense of what had happened. But he couldn't, he only felt increasingly confused, alarmed and out of control. He could feel the tree, the presence of it pressing into his awareness, trying to get his attention.

The tree was so kind, and he was in such turmoil. Without thinking, he intuitively answered the tree's invitation into its welcoming embrace. It enveloped him in a feminine care like that which he had felt in the girl's gaze – the same safe, beautiful feminine holding; a kind of love that he allowed to overwhelm him – and he fell back into her arms and let the tree take away all his fears.

33

The boy's name was Asaph and he worked for the oil merchant. He was strong and bright, keen and quick to learn. The oil merchant was jealous of his skills and attributes and instead of applauding him as an excellent worker, Asaph seemed to bring out the worst in him and he felt an overwhelming urge to keep the boy down. He wouldn't allow the boy to think he was special in any way, even though it was clear he was gifted. The merchant felt shown up somehow by the boy, and as Asaph shone, the merchant hardened against his Light and put it out at every opportunity. He refused to give the boy the pleasure of having pleased his master. The merchant chose to be unpleasant. It kept him in an artificial position of power. His age, his size, his authority the only power he had over the boy's never-ending wellspring of Light. And so, he chose to exert this power and crush the boy's spirit. He used his authority to extinguish whatever it was the boy had, his golden grain, which – at some deeper, unnameable level – the merchant feared.

Why was this boy so inwardly self-assured, so respectful, so bright, so... *good*? It made the merchant uncomfortable; it illuminated his own lack of goodness, and so it must be extinguished.

Asaph had worked for this man for many months. His father

had arranged everything. His father was in some way indebted to this man and so the merchant took his son to work for him. There was an arrangement in which the boy was the currency. The means of paying the debt.

Asaph didn't have a choice. He obeyed his father. There was no discussion. A forced indentured service to the merchant. Asaph resented this man and he resented his father for using him in this way. Resented that he must work off his fickle and uncaring father's debt for him.

And so, his bright innocence was challenged and eroded. He railed against the abuse of the merchant and against the cold, intractable nature of his father. He felt trapped. The harshness and brutality of these men he felt deeply. Some tender inner part of him longed to be seen and nurtured and honoured. His heart hurt. Was this the lot of a man? To ignore the tenderness and operate in the harshness. It weighed heavily on him.

And now this experience; the girl, the Light, the angel, the tree. The girl had seen his vulnerability and he had let her hold it, and somehow it had smashed open his heart and let the cosmos in. And that which had come through the girl, some feminine holiness, he began to find in the trees and the plants and the wind and the rocks. A living resource to hold his most vulnerable nature, soothe his anguish and restore his balance. And in his gratitude to Mother Earth, the land and the elements, he felt his own highest masculine aspect awaken as he appreciated her magic and bowed before the majesty of nature. He began to feel it everywhere – in the ground, in the animals and the trees. Even as he lifted the jars of olive oil and carried them against his chest, his heart seemed to move in time with the warm undulating gift of the olive trees inside.

After a few days, he found himself wandering back to where he had seen the girl. He wanted to see her again. He went to her dwelling house. He didn't know what he would say to the girl, but something in him wanted to acknowledge something in her. And so, he found himself hovering uncomfortably outside the house.

Heron's mother was inside. She was feeling heavy; the burden of her daughter's departure weighed heavily in her heart. It was a mother's selfless release of her child, a letting go, a loss, a trust. She saw the boy. He stood awkwardly but resolutely outside as if waiting, or hoping, or entreating in some way. She stepped outside and they stood together in front of the dwelling. Fragments of words left his mouth. The girl... the fight... he couldn't piece it together and the words seemed to wither as they left his mouth and landed in the field of pain that was the mother. The woman told him that Heron was not there; she had gone, and she didn't know if she would return.

He took in the information. It felt like a blow. Of all his imaginings of how this meeting might pan out, he hadn't imagined that she would be gone. It was as if a door had been closed just as it had been opened. He had seen a glimpse through the crack of an open door, enough to know what was there and enough to remember what he had seen. And then, slam! It was just a memory, a remembered imprint. He didn't understand it, but something deep within him knew her, knew what was through the door, and he wanted to go there.

He said thank you to the woman. He didn't know what for or why he was even there and, with his heart and mind swirling in confusion, he walked away. As he walked, the dusty ground beneath him seemed to part and in his mind's eye he felt he was walking under the surface of the Earth, in a channel with deep sides, a winding weaving pathway in the Earth. And he felt that if he just walked and walked and walked for long enough in the body of the Earth, he would find his way to her.

34

Asaph was in the room in which he spent much of his time. Jars of oil were all around. Different sizes, different types, different shapes. The room was dusty and dim. A narrow strip of sunlight, long and thin, stretched the length of the room up high close to the ceiling. A narrow horizontal slit filtering the only beam of light into the space. It created a thin blade of light, which illuminated the dancing dust particles. No one could see in or out. It was enough to illuminate the room, but not so much that the room would heat up and spoil the oil. This was Asaph's domain.

He knew how to take care of the oil. It was his job to grade the oil, decant it, measure it and organise the stock. Cruder oils were in large jars. Finer oils in smaller jars. He could tell by the smell, the viscosity, the colour, the clarity how to gauge the oil. And he became very skilled at his work. The merchant could leave him to it. Asaph had devised his own grading and refining methods and his own system of organisation. He was intelligent, thorough, efficient and capable. The boy enjoyed being proficient and doing the best job he could do. It gave him pleasure and pride to be so accomplished and he applied this aspect of his nature to every part of his labours.

He kept away from his master, the oil merchant, as much

as possible. The man was away for some of the time, or in the adjacent room from where he conducted business. The master could not be pleased, but Asaph took comfort in pleasing himself with his pursuit of excellence. It was a part of him that seemed to run the show now and drive him along, even if his domain for its expression was limited to a room full of oil jars.

He spent many long hours in that room. It was heavy work. The jars were cumbersome and their contents fickle in their fluidity. But he had quickly mastered handling them. He seemed to intuitively know the properties of things and the capacities of his own body. He knew the way things moved and worked – the mechanics of things. Weighing, measuring, calculating, it all came very naturally to him.

He was engrossed in his labours one day when, from the room next door, the merchant barked and summoned him. He didn't use the boy's name. He hadn't said it once in all those months. Did he even know what it was? He called him 'boy' in a way that emphasised his inferiority, reminded him of his place at every exchange.

Asaph tensed inside, braced himself and stepped out into the connecting room. It was much brighter there and it took a moment for his eyes to adjust. In the doorway stood a woman in long, dark robes. The sun that shone around her as she stood in the doorway looked to him like a kind of starburst. He wasn't sure whether the rays of light were coming from the sun as it illuminated her silhouette, or whether they actually emanated from the woman herself. It could have been either.

The normally coarse merchant stood swaying slightly. He became slippery like his oil as he smiled obsequiously at the woman in enquiry of her needs. The woman took a step forward from the doorway and Asaph could see her more clearly. What was it that held his attention? Her features were plain, but she had an air about her of self-possessed stillness; a kind of calm, steady, kind, safe, unshakable and mysterious strength. It impacted him and made him want to listen to what she had to say. It made him want to attend to her needs. He became alert, intent, and he awaited her request.

The merchant lowered himself onto his chair with a pained wince and reached for the stick that was never far from his hand. He leaned forward on it. He explained to Asaph that the woman was looking for their best oil. "Show the lady what we have," he said and he swept his arm through the air in a wide arc, proudly introducing her to his extensive stock. Jars stood shoulder to shoulder like soldiers lining the room. The woman glanced around, then looked at the boy. Their eyes met and something in her gentle, penetrating gaze made him feel seen at a deeper level. "I require some oil of the highest quality. Would you show me your purest oil?" Something about her made Asaph want to keep her to himself and to get her away from the oily merchant.

Asaph found himself saying that he had some very high-grade oil in the back room if she would like to see it. The merchant suddenly looked bored and dismissive. He grunted, rolled his eyes and shrugged his assent, and the woman followed the boy into the back room. Rarely did anyone enter his domain, his stronghold, what felt like his private world. The merchant usually left him to it; he dealt with business out the front. But here, Asaph felt he could relax and allow this woman to see his special place. In fact, he *wanted* her to see it, to see his organisation and skill and pride. He knew this woman had already seen this part of him and that she appreciated it.

She asked him his name. He replied and she told him that her name was Mariam. There was an ease between them. He found himself telling her about his father and the arrangement with the merchant, their deal, his bondage. How this room was his only zone of power. He could be excellent here in the confines of these four walls. He told her how that part of him burned to be excellent out in the world. He told her that he knew he was skilful, that he was good and that something burned within him to do good, to use his skills, his excellence to serve. He knew he had a much greater purpose than being confined here, trapped. He told her that, in the meantime, he would use this opportunity to be the best he could in this limited situation.

He looked around, seeing the room through the woman's eyes, someone who had never seen it before. And he was proud of his achievements under such unfavourable circumstances. It was as if he had refused to give up his dignity as his other liberties were taken away.

Mariam smiled at him. A smile that seemed to radiate from the bottom of her heart and not just her face. She reflected back her recognition of this part of him. She agreed it was hard to stay true to oneself, to take the higher road when those around you choose to align with lower aspects of themselves, to remain in the dense collective.

Her words made Asaph think of the cheap jars of oil. Huge quantities of thick, cloudy, unfiltered low-grade oil in the biggest jars. And it seemed fitting that this woman was in search of pure oil of the highest grade.

He felt a little vulnerable that he had shared so much with this stranger, but her smile reassured him and he composed himself. He wanted to give his best service to this woman. "Right, let me help you," he said and he knelt down and started dragging jars around. From a cool, dark corner, he pulled a stoppered jar. Its bulbous body was big enough to be held in his cupped palms. He presented it to Mariam with pride. This was his finest oil. He was keen to show her how clear it was, how golden and pure. But the woman didn't look at it. Instead, she took it in her hands and she closed her eyes. Mariam tuned in and felt the vibration of the oil. Indeed, it was very pure. It sang to her in gentle rhythms and she knew it was the perfect vehicle to hold the pure essence of the spikenard that she had distilled from the plant and which she carried with her in a tiny vial. She would mix the essence of the nard with the pure oil.

The pure oil seemed to hold something of the boy, too. Something of his devotion, his commitment, his willingness to excel. Something of the boy's uncrushable spirit, his innocence, his nobility, his golden grain. It was as if, during his many hours of dedication, filtering and nurturing and refining, the oil had absorbed something of the boy's spirit. She could feel it held within the vibration of the oil that she held in her hands.

Her heart smiled. This was perfect. Some vibration of Asaph, a high expression of his masculine nature was within the vibration of the oil. She knew she had been guided to the right place in coming here. It was perfect. Mariam knew that she would blend it with the liquid essence of the spikenard. The feminine vibration of the nard would be safe and her powers amplified by the vibration of the divine masculine that would carry her. The carrier oil for the nard. She smiled at the ingenuity of the universe. The feminine and masculine in perfect balance within the blended combination.

Her heart felt heavy. She knew she was being guided to prepare large quantities of the nard for anointing. She was following the inner nudges with a kind of inevitability and dread, and a painful acceptance of what she might need such quantities of the nard for. Her heart ached. She knew in her heart that it would be for her Yeshua. She did not know what lay ahead, but she knew this was a preparation, a process of putting things in place.

The boy had played his part beautifully and she marvelled at the wonder of it all. The innocent boy had no idea the part he was playing. How his essence, his own pure and excellent vibration, would play a part in what was to come.

35

Asaph was swept along with the crowds surging through the streets. Eventually, the crowd slowed and gathered at their destination. They stood a short distance from the men who were nailed to the crosses. Asaph was small and had pushed to the front as the crowd barged around him. The atmosphere, the crowd; everything felt electric. It was the man Yeshua they were all watching. He held their attention even though he didn't speak. Everyone was waiting, expecting him to say something. He was always delivering instruction, compelling people to see things differently, telling them, showing them with his miracles that there was more, there were answers, that this was not 'it'.

Asaph watched from the crowd. Why didn't he speak? he wondered. Asaph was entranced. He found that tears were quietly welling as he watched, transfixed by the man.

Women were there at the foot of the cross; they were allowed up close to Yeshua. He could see that the woman Mariam was there. He recognised her. The woman who had visited the oil merchant, who had taken his purest oil. The woman who had seen his golden grain, seen his Light. She was there, at the foot of the cross of Yeshua.

He watched her intently. He watched her connection to

Yeshua as he hung heavily above her on the cross. They seemed to be one. Asaph's vision shifted inwardly. His eyesight was blurred by his tears, but he didn't blink them away. He allowed the blurry screen to protect him from the sight, but at the same time it provided a screen against which an inner vision opened up. Another vision, an extension of the scene before him, another view.

And he felt as if part of him was with the man on the cross and the woman Mariam. He winced and held fast as his heart seemed to expand, stretching to its limit. Tears came and his head rolled with the intensity of it. His whole body expanded and he held strong with his feet planted in the Earth. Bigger and bigger, wider and wider, and each time his heart grew stronger. It was as if his heart were holding something, protecting something and he would not let go of it. Something in him knew to hold it, contain it, keep it there. Tears squeezed out as his whole being braced and expanded with the energies that roared through him. It was as if his life depended on holding steady, not giving in, not failing in this task.

What was he encompassing? He didn't know, but it was as if he were part of something that was happening between the woman, kneeling with her palms out and head back in front of the man who bled and hung his head down. He didn't know that his divine masculine essence was holding the woman of the nard as Mariam activated her.

Yeshua was bleeding, but Asaph was not connected to his physical body. The man and the woman were doing something outside of his body. Asaph could feel a vortex, a spiralling torrent of energy within the cage that was his heart. A swirling vortex going upwards from the density of Yeshua's bleeding body.

Asaph held firm; he held tight. His heart was breaking, but he held strong. He would not let go. He would hold this cage for the vortex, this upward spiralling of life force. His small body reeled, his head rolled and tears seemed to squeeze out of his heart as he used all of his duty, his nobility, his courage to hold on. It was as if he were holding, protecting, providing some essential structure for the movement of the man's spirit.

He stood there, buffeted by the people around him, and he didn't care that he was sobbing. The cage had held. The vortex was gone, and in the still and vast space, the altered atmosphere, the spanning of dimensions, he felt some masculine form lean forward and kiss him on the top of his head. It was as though Yeshua himself had kissed him on the head. Had blessed him, had anointed him with a sacred blessing that imprinted into his very essence.

36

As the years passed, Asaph continued to work for the oil merchant. As he became more and more skilled with the oils, the merchant hated him more and more. Asaph was supposed to be in oppressed servitude, some chattel of the merchant. And while the boy was obedient, he would not let the man grind him down. He chose to be positive and to go with the good as best he could and he became ever more accomplished. And the merchant became ever more bitter and hardened.

The more the boy refused to be broken, the more the merchant detested him. He grew older, lazier and increasingly cantankerous. He heaped more responsibility and labours onto the boy to crush him, but the boy just rose evermore.

The merchant wanted rid of the boy, but at the same time his business had come to depend on him. The merchant was stuck. Somehow, he had got himself into a corner. His greed for profits and his despising of the boy who now generated them for him was impossible for him to reconcile. He escaped his miserable dilemma by drinking increasing quantities of wine and, over time, the merchant became a raging drunk. He staggered about the place, swinging flasks of wine around as he ranted. He gorged on food and drink to blot out his rotten and festering feelings, and continued to project his increasing rage onto the boy. But the boy refused to take it on board, refused to relieve him of his darkness. And so, inwardly, the boy thrived and the oil merchant was eaten up by his own poison.

As time passed, Asaph increasingly covered for the declining merchant. He spoke to the buyers and took on more and more of the business and it blossomed as an extension of him, earning a good living for the merchant. And the merchant had nowhere to go with his predicament. Gradually, he became isolated, dense, inert, lost, like he had become a prisoner of his own self-loathing. It seemed that now the merchant was in bondage and Asaph was the free man.

In their arrangement, Asaph had few personal freedoms and yet he was free inside. The merchant had all the personal liberties afforded a wealthy free man and yet he was inwardly incarcerated. It was as if a balance was tipping.

Asaph looked at the merchant one day. A drunken, snoring heap collapsed in his chair in the front room of the store. He sprawled, reclined, his belly distended and his form propped on outstretched swollen legs. His physical form seemed engorged with a kind of inner festering rot. Asaph watched quite objectively; he didn't feel very much at all. He regarded the huge bulk, with his fat belly rising and falling in time with his rasping snores. His neck was heavy with folds of flesh, which seemed to crush the very breath out of him, and his body jerked and fought for air. What a waste, Asaph thought as he watched the man. It was safe to watch and contemplate the merchant now that he was beached in his chair, incapable and impotent in a drunken stupor. His vast body seemed to be consuming him, taking him ever deeper into his own darkness, as if his own body were chewing up his very essence until he was completely lost.

The boy studied him and pondered. These days, the man was barely able to function. Asaph had been propping up the business, covering for the merchant. He had tried to help him by setting an example of a different way of being. Asaph knew he had done all he could.

In contrast to the merchant's decline, Asaph had grown into a strong and lean seventeen-year-old. A young man skilled in business and bright of heart and he felt the pull of the door to the outside world. He looked at the door. He looked at the merchant. He had done his duty. He had done enough. He owed him nothing. They were even.

The energy outside the door was expansive, alive, exciting, a moving stream of possibility. The merchant and his oil emporium on this side of the threshold felt dense, rigid, constricting and stifling.

It was time. Something burned in the boy's heart, a pull to a bigger stage. A stage on which he knew he could play a part, although what part, he had no idea. It seemed easy all of a sudden, like a scale gently tipping, and there was nothing to stop him walking out of the door into his freedom. It felt as though it was the simplest thing in the world.

He owed nothing to his father; he owed nothing to the merchant. His conscience was clear. The slate was clean and he looked again at the door. He remembered the woman Mariam, the woman who had bought his purest oil, the woman he had seen with Yeshua that day, years ago, on the cross. He remembered her standing in that same doorway the day she came to the store. How she stood in that portal, on that same threshold with her golden rays. And as he remembered her standing there, he felt a pull to the doorway. It was as if the memory of her divine feminine Light was magnetising him forward to it. And with its lure came the full knowledge that everything would be alright.

As he stepped into the doorway, he felt as though Mariam herself was there flooding some kind of sacred blessing upon him. He was held in a pulsing golden ball of light and again he felt the unconditional love that had exuded from the woman when they had crossed paths all those years before. He felt her arms wrap around him, holding him in the safest loving embrace, and he knew that everything would be okay. He allowed the Light to infuse him. As he surrendered himself into it, it washed away any remaining doubts and lingering guilt about what he was doing. Her love permeated through all of his wounds. His father's rejection of him. The merchant's humiliation and ridicule of him, and the years of aggression and exploitation. Their stains were cleansed by this feminine Light.

When Asaph stepped forward through the doorway, he felt renewed, honoured and seen by her Light. The blessing of this woman's unconditional love upheld him and inspired him. He knew the grace of woman and he stepped forward into the unknown, a free man.

37

saph walked towards the lights in the distance, towards the town. The warm glow of the light from the dwelling houses made him think of the warmth of his old home, of his mother. He thought of his childhood and how he felt about his mother. He remembered her warmth, her warm arms and soft skin as she held him and bathed his cuts and bruises as a little boy. How, as a child, he would run home after a scrape, knowing that once he got to her, everything would be alright. Like magic, she made things better.

It was similar to what he had felt from the feminine Light in the doorway earlier. The same magic, and now all he wanted to do was to see his mother again. It suddenly seemed the most pressing thing and so he started to pick his way through the familiar streets and alleys he had played in as a child. He was surprised he could still remember the way. The years in between hadn't diminished his imprinted mental map of the maze of streets and alleyways.

It was dusk and his pace slowed. He was close to home. He moved silently between the dwellings. He could hear the muted sounds of family life inside them.

Suddenly, he felt anxious. For a moment, he remembered his father, uncaring, hard-hearted and thick-skinned. But his thoughts were swept aside by the more urgent and pressing ones of his mother. He imagined watching her through a window. He imagined her cooking. He was hungry and he wanted his mother to feed him. He wanted her nourishment in all of her ways. His stomach ached for her cooking and his heart ached for her mother love.

As he allowed himself to think of her care, her motherliness, her mother to his son, he filled with a sudden unease. He didn't know what he would find or how he would be received. He had not seen her for so many years, not since he was a boy and was sold off by his father. There had been nothing she could do. She had obeyed her husband. But Asaph knew by the way she had clasped him tight and by the tears that swam in her eyes that his being sent away was not her wish; it was her lot and she had to accept it, as must he.

Slowly, he approached the house he had grown up in. It was crammed in tightly between others. He remembered the neighbours in the adjoining homes. The other mothers. Feeding, they were always feeding. When they weren't holding a baby to their milky breasts, they were cooking and feeding and nourishing their children. He had been one of those children the last time he was here. All those he had played with would be grown up now. It was different, but also the same as he remembered.

His heart was loud in his chest. The anxiety and excitement were a heady mix. He inched closer. He waited. He could see a lamp through the window opening. The shutter was still open and the lamp glowed inside. Outside, it became darker and he became invisible. His eyes were fixed on the lamp. Had his mother lit it? Was she inside? A knot tightened in his heart. The lamp flickered. He thought of the oil that was sending up a smoky flame. He knew the kind of oil that burned like that with a rich golden flame and threads of black smoke. He could tell it was full of impurities. He was mesmerised by the flickering glow; it calmed him.

And then he saw her. It was only for a moment. She came to the window and closed the small shutter door across its opening. His heart leapt. It was just long enough to see her outline, her shape, her movement. And something inside him cracked and tears ran down his face. He couldn't stop them. This woman, this mother, what was it that made him cry? What was it, in seeing her, that made him collapse inside and feel small and vulnerable? How did this work? How did his mother do this just by being his mother?

It was as if the boy who had been sent away had armoured himself from the pain of her loss and that armour was now crumbling at the sight of her. He was helpless to stop the flow of tears as his heart opened again to the possibility of her. The long-repressed possibility of his mother.

The waves gradually subsided and Asaph began to feel more composed. All he wanted to do now was hold onto her, reunite, and know that everything would be okay.

Asaph was very hungry; he hadn't eaten in a long time and his stomach felt hollow and empty. It was this more than anything that gave him the impetus, the courage to stand at the door and knock.

He gently banged his hand on the door. "It's me, Asaph. It's Asaph," he called. There was no sound from inside. He waited. His heart lurched. He knew she was inside. Is she ignoring me? The thought cut him deeply. "Mother, it's me, Asaph," he called more urgently.

Inside, the woman heard the voice calling. Was she imagining it? Then, she heard it again. Asaph. She stood up and moved slowly towards the door. She placed a palm on the door as though she was feeling whether it was true that her son was on the other side of it. There was another bang. She started. She was frightened suddenly. Frightened of what it would mean for the boy. He couldn't come in. His father would not be happy.

It had all been about the oil, the business with the merchant. Her husband had owed him money. She didn't understand the details of it, what had gone on between her husband and the merchant, but the threats he made to her family at that time came back to her as if it were yesterday. It had been a bad time. The merchant had threatened to turn their house into a fireball. He wanted what he was owed. She had been terrified and so Asaph going to him had been the price of their safety. And now Asaph was at the door and this could only be bad. It reignited her memories. She had to give up her son to stay safe. And so having him here felt dangerous. The fear gripped her and dominated any other emotions. She wanted to keep the door closed, to stay safe, to keep things as they were, and yet some small, deep part of her heart wanted to open it, too.

"Mother?" The word came through the door. It was her boy. As if acting by themselves, against her better judgement, her hands seemed to reach out and they opened the door a fraction. In the dim light that glowed from inside the house, she saw his face. It was that of a young man. He was so tall, as tall as her, taller maybe. She gasped and held her fingers tight to her lips as if to stop something from pouring out.

Her love for him swept over her and she held out her arms. They held each other in tearful waves of incredulity, relief and joy.

"Do you have anything to eat?" asked Asaph. He stepped inside and her dreams were complete as she plied him with the very best she could find.

38

His father was pacing around the room. The morning had come and the atmosphere was altered. The joy had been replaced by tension. Asaph sat with his legs astride and body wide open on a chair. He wasn't afraid of his father now. The intervening years had given his father a paunch and deeper lines on his face, but his demeanour was unchanged. The man continued to pace and the tension increased, the anger brewed. Asaph sat with his heart wide and strong. He knew his own strength and he knew his own worth. It was as if his inner strength was spreading out from his heart across his chest like an armoured breastplate. He had no fear.

His mother was restless and jittery. Nervously, she busied herself and wished all this would stop. The hostility that was in the air, the prospect of the clashing of her men; it was terrifying and unbearable. She interjected with placating words and gestures. She stood between them with her palms out low, trying to hold down the violent eruption she sensed was brewing. She pleaded with her husband, but he ignored her as if she wasn't even there. Her efforts at conciliation brushed away without him even looking at her.

The man's brow was lowered and set, his jaw rigid, and his anger rose. Asaph remained seated, heart strong in the armoured breastplate of his own truth. It seemed his best defence and it held strong in the face of the hostility that was growing and coming in his direction. Asaph watched the man operate. He could see that his father needed to use him to take on all his own failings, his own shortcomings and somehow make his son responsible for all his unacknowledgeable flaws. His failings as a man, as a father. He could accept no wrongdoing on his part for what he had done all those years before. He bolstered himself with feelings of entitlement and self-righteousness. He reinforced his own stories that Asaph's bondage was justified. He was the father, the patriarch; he had the power and that's just how it was.

Asaph was no longer the obedient unquestioning child he had been. He watched his father and saw him now for what he was. A bully. A pathetic, weak bully, who had sold his own son to relieve his debt. A debt to the merchant of his own making, from his own bad judgment and weakness. His scheming had somehow gone wrong and the solution was simple: to use his own son, to use his own flesh and blood to save his skin, to escape the responsibilities of his own actions.

Asaph had not expected this. His father's refusal to take responsibility. His determination to make his son wrong and himself right and a contemptuous disrespect started to brew in Asaph. It burned at the edges of his breastplate.

Asaph had survived the intervening years by not brooding on how he had become a servant to the merchant. It had been too painful to dwell on, so he chose to keep himself busy excelling and pleasing where he could.

Even as he walked back to his childhood home the previous night, he had barely thought of his father. It had been the thought of his mother that had pulled him back, her warmth like the rays in the doorway activating his desire, his need to reconnect to her. And now this was satisfied, the spectre of his father loomed before him.

Asaph's heart was burning; the pain of his father's rejection, the years of suppressed hurt licked at the edges of his breastplate. His father's value of him as an expendable trading token. How he must have slept at night with no thought or care for what had become of his son. Beneath Asaph's armour, a volcano was rumbling. His father's lack of remorse was stoking the belly of the volcano. He watched the man silently pacing, anger fermenting, face tight and twitching, fingers clenched and jaw tensing.

The man's growing fury was now matched by Asaph's own growing incandescence. Asaph's body burned as if the current of his life force, the golden Light that propelled him through his incarceration, was changing. Every cell of his being was instead running through with filaments of fire. Of burning righteous holy rage. The sparks jumped through his body; the flames licked and swirled like a vortex in his heart. A fireball began to course through him, gathering pace, gathering power as he watched his father. His father's lack of repentance stoked the fire. Not a hint of remorse for sending him away from his mother, his home, his life into the hands of a man who would torch a house for the price of a few shekels.

Suddenly, all the abuse, derision, humiliation, brutality and beatings of the merchant came into laser-sharp focus. Each of the blows he had endured had been taken for his father. And now that man paced before him after all this time, with nothing but blame and anger towards him.

Asaph hated him, hated him for what he had done. In the intervening years, when he had thought of his father's actions, he had tried to understand, tried to forgive, tried to see the bigger picture, hoped in some way for resolution in some unknown future. An apology, a reckoning, some remorseful self-reflection by his father, a way forward. This had been Asaph's hope.

And it was only now, when he was faced with its absence, that he realised how much he had leaned on that hope to get him through. And now he knew it had been a false hope, a figment of his imagination, some innocent childlike wish for a happy ending. It was all rushing through him now. He had used this hope to prop himself up and protect himself from the pain of what his father had done. And without it, without the protection from the truth, without the fantasy that sustained him, the dregs of his self-delusion were now burning off in the crucible of his heart, like the impurities in the burning oil leaving in black, wispy tendrils as they transformed to reveal the excruciating truth.

He could see clearly now and he loathed this man. He despised his well-fed paunch from a life of ease and living off the backs of others. Using those around him, using his mother, skulking around, scoring deals, always on the make. He had never done anything through honest hard work.

Asaph's burning rage seemed to suddenly crystallise into an icy clarity. It was as if the fiery rage was built up like a ball of fuel, the propulsion, the force behind a new focused clarity, a kind of white blindness.

He heard nothing; his mother was pulling at his arm, but he didn't feel her. He rose to his feet. He was in a cool, icy white tunnel within himself. His father stopped pacing and looked at him with alarm. His panicked expression didn't register in Asaph's white blindness. He saw his father's face and he felt nothing in response to his look of terror.

Asaph held the knife in his right hand. He was in a heightened, sharpened state, focused, honing in. His laser focus came with a deadening – a blinkering that filtered out his mother's screams and his father's supplications. His father was backing off now, his palms raised by his head, incredulous, terrified. His mother was screaming and pulling at him, but it didn't penetrate his white rage. He didn't shake her off, he didn't feel her, he just kept moving down the white tunnel towards his father.

He watched his father's whimpering cowardice, heard his begging pleas as he staggered backwards. Asaph felt nothing and kept moving forwards. His father stumbled backwards onto the floor. He lay writhing and scrabbling on his back. It was pathetic.

Asaph looked into his father's eyes as he leaned over him, holding up the knife. He was steely and emotionless. Asaph leaned in and pressed the blade against the man's throat. He watched the point indent the flesh of his neck. The flesh glistened with sweat. He played with the pressure on his throat as his father gulped and gasped. His cowardly begging eyes met Asaph's cold, intractable and unyielding gaze. The man's bowels evacuated and his bladder released and he trembled, whimpered and pleaded for mercy with his eyes into those of his son. The knife was pressing hard against his flesh. For several torturous moments, Asaph held it there. Asaph had complete power and his father had none.

Asaph could smell the man's excrement, his rank sweat. His revulsion at his father was complete. The man squirmed with his palms up beside his head in surrender. Asaph pressed the blade down flat on his father's throat, constricting his breathing with its pressure. He pressed harder, the man's eyes bulged and he choked and gagged. Asaph held it there. Time stood still. He looked into his father's eyes and in their glassy depths he saw a vision of a small boy. He saw his father as a small boy, being beaten by his father. He saw the pattern. His father, his father's father and his father before him. A line of fathers beating their sons. Fathers' brutality to sons. It was all there, crystallised in the terrified eyes of his father. And Asaph understood. He saw the cycles of violence in men, the crushing of the tender boys in each of them. The beautiful little boys, the sweet innocent boys, each born with their golden grain of innate goodness, each abused and crushed and their gentleness obliterated, perpetuating the pattern, imprinting it into the next generation.

The chime of this truth seemed to crack the blinkering white walls of his rage. The walls collapsed inwards and his awareness flooded back in. It was enough.

He held onto his father's eyes and the vision he had seen in them and he released the pressure of the blade. He lifted it off his father's throat and dropped the knife on the floor. He could hear his mother weeping. Asaph got to his feet. His father was sobbing like a child, broken and helpless.

Asaph walked out of the door. He breathed the air in deeply and walked away. He was shaking and his feelings engulfed him. Retribution, justice, the urge for violence, alarm at his own capacity for violence, shame.

It was hard to be a man.

39

Asaph walked away from the house. The sun was still low in the sky and the heat of the day was some hours away, so it was easy to walk. He thought to himself that he would just walk until it became too hot and then he would stop and regroup. But for now, he just wanted to walk away, further and further, putting more and more distance between himself and the house, the events, the ugliness.

The air felt unusually cool. The breeze refreshed him, cooled his fiery nerves, and he was grateful for it. The memory returned to him of the day when he was connected to the tree; how he had then found comfort and strength in a connection to the natural world. When did he forget that? How did that get covered over, buried, forgotten? He remembered that day. The girl who had awoken something in him with her eyes; how he felt as though the elements, the trees, the rocks were like his friends. How he was aware of his own connection to the Earth and how magical and *right* it had felt.

He had dismissed it, he supposed. There was no place for such things in the hard labours of his life with the merchant. It was not a thing he had ever heard spoken of by others. His life had been more a fight for survival, a more urgent need to keep going, and in time he had forgotten the experience.

But as the unusually cool breeze quenched the remnants of the fire that had erupted in him, he remembered. He felt as if he were part of the breeze, as if he were the breeze. And it was supportive, approving, encouraging as if it were telling him to keep his chin up, that he wasn't alone, that it would be okay. He didn't understand the sensation in the wind, but he was so fractured and scattered that he took it at face value as some show of support and he was grateful to it.

He was able to gather himself and steady himself. He knew he would not return to his family home. He thought of the old neighbours, people he had known from his childhood, perhaps he would seek out some old connections. But that felt empty, like going backwards. He thought of the people he had met through working for the oil merchant – customers, other traders – but something in him withered at the thought of pursuing these connections. It was all tainted with his past.

He felt his strength was in his aloneness somehow, where his intuition was most alive. He liked who he was; he valued himself in spite of it all. He stopped and stood still. Something made him stop. A dusty track was beneath his feet. Scrubby landscape surrounded him. He could hear insects buzzing. A donkey cart rattled by, kicking up clouds of dust into the breeze.

He stood motionless, relaxed, and the ground beneath him seemed to come alive. A deep, all-knowing mother and he heard her say, "Give it to me." He closed his eyes and, in his confusion, he surrendered into her and he gave his heaviness to her. He felt the pulse of his troubles pump downwards into her vastness. The moment passed. He felt different, lighter. Had the Earth really taken away his heaviness? His heart felt stronger, more emboldened, as if this Mother of the Earth had his back and was an ally.

He shook his head and opened his eyes. It seemed illogical

and ridiculous, yet at the same time it had felt real. He gave a kind of awkward smile to whatever this was. And in his rudderless life, his aloneness, his uncertainty, it seemed to provide him with an anchor and a compass. It was all he had.

40

The sun was gradually getting higher in the sky and Asaph was lost in thought as he continued along the roadway. Suddenly, through the haze of his reverie, he was aware of a man coming towards him and, without warning, the man lurched forward and punched him square in the face. Asaph was sent reeling. It was unprovoked, out of nowhere. The man just approached him and struck one huge forceful blow straight into his face. Asaph's jaw cracked, his lights seemed to go out and he found himself on the ground, such was the force of the blow. He had barely seen the man; he had come from nowhere. Asaph had had a sense of blue clothing and a glimpse of a man older than him, with thick whiskers on the sides of his cheeks. And then, smash.

He was in pain. His jaw was ringing from the blow and his head from the impact with the ground. He lay panting heavily and groaning. It had been a swift blow from a fist. The merchant had preferred a stick to hit and poke him with, as if he was an animal. This was man to man, flesh to flesh, fist to jaw.

He lay on his back on the roadside. The sun was bright on the other side of his closed lids. He tried to open them, but the dazzling sun and the ringing in his head was too much. As he lay winded, he was aware that his assailant was standing in front of him. It was as if he was waiting for Asaph to recover himself. Asaph sensed the threat from the man was gone. He was just standing there, legs astride, hands by his sides, waiting; he wasn't going to go away.

Asaph pulled himself up so he was sitting on the ground with his head held in his hands. The breath that had been punched out of him was returning and the reverberations in his head seemed to stabilise in the cradle of his hands. His fingers spread from his jaw to his temples like a brace. He opened his mouth and moved his jaw from side to side, assessing the damage. It throbbed with pain, but seemed to still function as it should.

Gradually, he blinked open his eyes. His vision was blurry and the sun was too bright, but he made out the man's legs in a blue robe before him. It seemed to take several minutes of recovery before Asaph could keep his eyes open, before they would focus and he could regain his composure and wherewithal. Meanwhile, the man was just standing, unthreatening, calm and waiting.

Asaph rolled to move to his feet. The man offered him his hand. Something made Asaph take it and he was helped to his feet. The man's face was smiling as Asaph looked into it. He had soft dark whiskers on the sides of his face and above his lip, and he was smiling a crooked smile, showing uneven teeth and something about him was familiar. Asaph regarded him cautiously as he rubbed his aching jaw. The man was now grinning. Asaph could see that he was no older than himself and all at once Asaph recognised him. They had known each other from years before. Asaph had punched that face himself years before. He had seen that smile back then and had wanted to punch it right off the boy's genial, grinning face.

They looked at each other in a growing realisation. "Now we are even," said the young man, smiling. He was actually chuckling. What a caper this was. Asaph had punched him and pummelled him and left him sprawling in the dust all those years before. Asaph had been victorious, full of swagger and bravado until he had walked over to the girl who was watching the fight, and she had looked into his eyes that day. The day he felt struck through by starlight from the Gods and the angel had connected him to the tree.

How strange, Asaph thought, that he was just thinking about that long-forgotten day and the impact it had had on him. And now this. How strange. The coincidence seemed uncanny. Asaph saw that, indeed, their business had not been finished from that day. And that now it was. He had now received what he had given out. He had a sneaking respect for this young man in front of him. And Asaph couldn't help but smile, too.

The pair of them grinned and chuckled at the fairness of it somehow; the acknowledgment of setting things straight, settling the score. The young man rubbed his knuckles and swivelled his aching wrist. The blow had jarred and hurt it. It was clear he didn't make a habit of using his fists. His face crumpled in acknowledgment of the pain he felt in his hand and Asaph laughed.

Some bond of understanding, an appreciation of the fairness, the equity, an even deal was mutually recognised. Some fraternity had been born of that noble punch to right the order of things.

They walked together side by side. The whiskered young man allowing for Asaph's slow pace as he found his balance, unsteadily putting one foot in front of the other. Asaph found him easy company; open and light and bright of heart. He was soft and rounded at the edges and Asaph guessed that in the intervening years his labours had not been as physical as his own and that food had been more plentiful, and that joy had been more free-flowing. At the side of his levity and good humour, Asaph felt the contrasting weight of his own life. Yet there was something in this cheerful young man that he liked. A kindness, a sort of simple childlike kindness. He was a bit ungainly, a bit awkward and gauche in his manner, but he held no grudge. He had simply levelled the score and that was that. And Asaph liked that.

Asaph walked comfortably by his side. He was lean and muscular and sharp at the side of this soft-bodied, kind, and fundamentally cheerful acquaintance. He had an innocence that Asaph felt slightly protective of. At one time, he had wanted to punch that out of him and now he wanted to protect it. He pondered that strange shift. How could that be?

His new friend – could he call him a friend? – chatted easily about his life and family. He had several sisters and they all spoiled him. He was the only boy and he was the eldest. His mother doted on him and his father thought he could do no wrong. Almost to the point of delusion, the boy admitted with a mischievous grin.

And so it was that Asaph came to spend the night in his new friend's home. The mother and sisters were as welcoming as he had been told to expect. So many sisters – six or seven, eight maybe; a gaggle, a squall of giggling, squabbling bustling females. The father just threw his hands up. He was heavily outnumbered. It was a theatrical gesture of submission, of kindly exasperation and acceptance of their dominance in the household. It was this scene that Asaph walked into. The father greeted him warmly, glad of another man to redress the balance.

The three men talked late into the evening. Their bellies full and their needs met by the endlessly chattering, clattering, chiding, providing, serving women, powerful in the stronghold of their domestic duties.

It was clear this family was very different from his own. There was no violence in the men. There was no fear in the women. Any shouting and giving of orders came from the mother as she captained the ship of her family. This father, this son; they were a revelation to Asaph. Comfortable and even affectionate with each other; interested in the world and in people and in how Asaph had come to be eating with them that night.

Asaph didn't reveal too much. He didn't want to disrupt the ambience with the drama of his own story. He didn't want to alienate them. He didn't want to tell them that earlier that day, he had held a knife to the throat of his own father. He didn't want to dwell on why he deserved the punch.

He reflected on the kindness of his new friend. There were no ties, no conditions; he was simply sharing his bounty with one he could see was less fortunate. The deep tensions, the violence and power-play Asaph had known were absent here. There was enough for everyone. Enough of what? he wondered. The house was not opulent and the food was ordinary, but there seemed to be plenty of something. Good will, kindness, laughter – whatever it was, it softened Asaph and he felt received, welcomed and safe.

41

In the morning, the father took Asaph the short walk across to a nearby low building. There were piles of fleeces. Sheep fleeces, heaps and heaps of them. The smell was pungent. It was gloomy and dusty, and in the airless room, the aroma was overpowering. Asaph put his hand over his face. The father seemed unaffected by the smell as he good-naturedly explained the process of preparing the wool. Removing brushwood debris, insects and larvae; soaking the fleeces to clean them. Outside, two boys were pushing the fleeces under water with big sticks, submerging them in large troughs.

The boys stood on benches so they could reach above the deep troughs. The father introduced them to Asaph and gave a brief resume of their character and circumstances. Asaph anticipated their tension, their fear at the appearance of their master, but he realised it was his own imprint, his own memory of the oil merchant that made him flinch and tense with vigilance on their behalf.

The boys carried on as the father chattered to Asaph. It was heavy work. They dragged the wet fleeces from trough to trough and then pulled them out onto a table of what looked like intersecting laths, and he watched the boys pressing the fleeces to squeeze and drain the water from them. He could see more battens on which the fleeces were spread out to dry in the sun.

Asaph listened and watched on. This is what the man did. Bought fleeces, prepared them and sold them on. This was his business. Already Asaph could see there must be a better way to extract the water from the fleeces. It was inefficient to have a boy pressing and squeezing, and his sharp mind was imagining a wooden press of some sort, under pressure somehow to squash and extrude in one simple motion. This was how Asaph's mind worked. He could see inefficiencies, limitations, problems, and he felt compelled to find solutions, improve things, raise things up.

The father was still chattering away and led Asaph inside to where his friend was sitting at a table counting money. He heard them approach and grinned at Asaph as he placed piles of coins in pouches. He seemed to be in his element. It was clear to see that his friend's gifts did not lie in the manhandling of heavy, rancid sheep fleeces. The father instructed his son to take Asaph with him today. They were going to buy more fleeces. The friend grinned his lopsided smile and his eyes sparkled. Asaph warmed to him more and more.

At the animal market, free-roaming chickens flapped and squawked in alarm. Others were in crates; goats bleated, their long ears swinging as they trotted along. Sheep were being herded, and donkeys and mules were tied to posts. Some donkeys were old and thin, ravaged by hard labour and looking only fit for slaughter. A braying mule stamped its frustration, hooves pawing at the ground, head weaving from side to side.

Asaph's friend cheerily led him through the suffocating fug of the hot animals, piles of droppings and clouds of flies. They came to an enclosure full of sheep, heavy with their scraggy woollen coats. Their black faces and marble eyes all looked identical to Asaph.

His friend stood with his hands on his hips, his soft belly protruding above his fingers, and with ill-concealed delight, he surveyed the sight before him. Skilled men and boys picked off sheep one by one, dragging them into a pen and wrestling the animals to the ground. They flipped them over with such confidence, any resistance or struggle from the animal was nullified and the sheep reclined on their backs, helpless and ready to give up their woolly coats.

Asaph watched wide-eyed at the skill of the men and boys as they clipped and sheared the fleeces from the sheep. The wool fell away in great chunks as if they were peeling it off, like peeling the skin of an orange, leaving their pithy white bodies clean and fresh and unblemished beneath.

As the last piece was clipped away and fell to the floor, the sheep was released. It righted itself and shook and staggered off, newly naked on stick-thin legs. The fleece was thrown over the edge of the pen into a donkey cart and this is how the fleeces were sold, by the cartload. Several cartloads had built up and stood in a row.

"Follow me," said Asaph's friend, smiling, and he raised an eyebrow in a conspiratorial gesture. Asaph smiled back and watched his friend begin his performance. He assumed a suddenly serious countenance as he walked up and down, surveying the row of carts and their dense, spongy, filthy contents. He assessed them with a look of disapproval. He made great play of poking a stick into them, parting the fleeces, checking that the shepherd had not only placed the finest ones on top. He dug down with his stick, making disapproving grunts, and glanced at the shepherd. They had done business before. Then, with a wink at Asaph, he turned and walked away.

This apparently was all part of the game and his friend clearly enjoyed it. He told Asaph there was an art to getting the best deal with these shepherds, and Asaph delighted in watching his friend's good-natured acting. The shepherd had noted the young man's interest. The cord between buyer and seller had been strung. Walking away had only increased the tension on the cord.

Presently, with the raise of an eyebrow, the friend resumed his serious expression and returned casually to the carts. He lifted the stinking fleeces with his stick, rubbing them between his fingers, gauging the quality. The shepherd threw another fleece onto the cart. Droppings clung to its blackened knotted fringes, which draped over the edge of the wagon. The shepherd was out of breath and rested both hands and his chin upon his staff before the buyer.

Asaph watched the theatre unfold. His friend expressed concerns about the quality of the goods. The shepherd was affronted, asserted their worth and shook his head in disbelief at the price offered. His friend shrugged and quietly turned away; a loss of interest, a snort at the shepherd's price, a tightening of the cord. A retraction, a bartering by the seller. He could take a little less. "How much less?" pressed his friend with renewed interest.

The sheep bleated, sweat dripped from the shepherd's burnished brow. He wiped it with the back of his hand. He paused and drank deeply from a leather flask, prolonging the drama as he considered his options. He needed to shift these fleeces. Half of his flock remained unshorn. Two boys continued to fill the carts. He had a glut, a surfeit, his annual harvest was plentiful.

He lowered his price; he was doing the buyer a favour. The buyer bit his lip and gave out a long sigh and he contorted his mouth into a pained grimace as if chewing on something unpleasant as he ruminated on the offer.

The buyer said he would take all four carts if that fifth one was thrown in with the price and he waved a hand at the newly filled cart. He knew he was pushing his luck. It was verging on an insult. It stung, but the shepherd expected nothing less from this buyer. It was a good effort on the buyer's part – a bold counter. The shepherd played for time. The buyer raised an eyebrow at the shepherd and allowed a knowing smile to turn up one side of his mouth. The shepherd knew he had been pinned; his flexibility exposed. He parried with an offer of the reduced price and half an extra cart.

The deal was struck, a bargain made. They shook hands, money was exchanged and his friend turned and walked away. Somehow, he had arranged delivery of the fleeces. It was impressive. They watched a boy hitch a donkey to the cart. It was clear to Asaph that his friend would not be doing any of the physical toil if he could avoid it.

His friend seemed in no hurry to return home to business. From his money pouch, he took a few coins and purchased a selection of fruit from the market. As the fleece carts rumbled off to their destination, Asaph and his friend found a place to sit and together they ate the food. Asaph wasn't used to eating in the daytime, but his friend urged him, pushing fruit at him with an encouraging grin. "A celebration," he said between mouthfuls, "of a good deal," and he lifted the fruit aloft in a kind of victory salute, before merrily feasting on the juicy bounty.

It struck Asaph how unashamed his friend was to enjoy the abundance of life and his generous desire to share it with him. A kind of enjoyment ran through his friend, an unabashed delight at life, an apparently irrepressible joy at the smallest things. Asaph slowly chewed a date while his friend wiped juice and fruity flesh from his whiskers. If not exactly contagious, his levity and delight felt, at least, refreshing and liberating. His friend had enjoyed the fun of the barter, the pleasure of a good deal. Asaph suspected that even if it had been a bad deal, his friend would still somehow have found something to celebrate in it.

Asaph sat in contemplation at the new situation he found himself in. It was as if some of his own heavy coat, the knotted matted burden of his past oppression, was peeling away like the heavy coat of the sheep to reveal a fresh start, a soft naked underbelly. And like the sheep, he could now grow a new coat. He could see he now had an opportunity to start afresh and grow a different coat.

42

And so it came to be that Asaph stayed with his friend and was absorbed into his family. He worked with the fleeces by day and ate his meals with the family in the evening, and later returned to sleep on a thin mattress on the floor at the fleece sheds. He became accustomed to the smell of the fleeces and was grateful to have a home and an outlet for his creativity and his problem-solving as he worked diligently in the business. He sharpened up the processes, brought in new ideas and he was content.

His friend was unshakable in his resolute positivity and a great camaraderie blossomed between them. They respected each other's talents and together they were a formidable team. Asaph's practical skills, his vision, his dedication and enterprise, and his friend's astute and silver-tongued charm with traders soon brought rewards for the business.

Seasons passed and Asaph thrived. His days took on a purposeful rhythm; he was appreciated and the family welcomed him as one of their own. He found that as he ate with the family, among the raucous chatter, his attention was taken more and more by one of the sisters.

What was it about her? he wondered as he watched her over the months turning from a girl to a young woman. Her sisters babbled and frothed like the surface of a stream, while in her, he sensed the depth of an ocean. Her ocean pulled on him. He found himself watching her one evening, her elbows propped on the table as she tore the bread. She held it, turning it absently in her fingers while her sisters greedily stuffed their share into their mouths. He found he began to try to impress her, talking about his achievements in the business, his ideas and innovations. He couldn't help himself; it just came out in an involuntary flustered response to her beguiling presence.

The girl was not immune to the effect she had on Asaph. And, in return, she admired him and indeed cared about him. Her heart felt soft and it seemed to reach across the table to him with her dreamy glance through her gentle eyes. He received it. Her care and appreciation had landed in the tenderness of his own heart and it undid him, unravelled him and made him feel exposed. What was a man to do with this strange entanglement of feelings? He wanted her gaze. It was like a prized and intoxicating liquor. One drop of the liquor made him feel special, invincible and like he could do anything. At the same time, one drop of the liquor made his limbs go weak and his face flushed. His throat constricted and blocked his words, and as she looked at him, he oscillated between feeling like a king and a small boy.

His thoughts became preoccupied with her. His absent moments were spent recalling her face, her soft stillness, her graceful arms, as slender and silky as ribbons. Her hair was long and her eyes were clear and still, and seemed to be able to see into the deeper reaches of his being. Like her sisters, she joined in the family chatter and carried out her chores. But there was an inner serenity about her. Her nerves didn't seem so frayed and she was less animated than her sisters. Amid the bustling of the gaggle of women, she had something different. A self-possession, a kind of self-knowing, a quality he couldn't define with his mind and clever words. Although he tried to describe it, it was something that could only be felt.

His friend was quick to notice their mutual attraction. Was it that obvious? He presumed his inner tumult was invisible as he went about his daily tasks. His friend teased him, just for the sport of seeing him cringe and bluster in his denials, and feigned nonchalance. But he grinned. Happy for his friend and happy for his sister and happy for this frisson of excitement in the family.

And so, in time, it was arranged. A marriage. It suited everyone. The father would retain Asaph in the business. His hard work and improvements were already reaping financial reward for his family. A small dwelling would be built adjoining the fleece building, a short walk down the track. Asaph would still be on hand for the business and his daughter would live with him there.

In the months that led up to the wedding, Asaph felt like the luckiest man in the land. The pain of his own parents and his years with the oil merchant were behind him. He had a place in the world, a job, a family and now he would take a bride. He was nineteen.

It was a happy wedding. The women had prepared a feast, and wine and beer flowed. The celebrations and music went on long into the evening. This girl had been given to him by her father. The man approved of Asaph; he valued him, and his daughter felt like the greatest gift. He knew the man saw her as one of his many daughters he must marry off, but Asaph willingly took her as his. The father impressed upon him that she was now his responsibility, his chattel, his woman.

Asaph looked across at the revellers in the dusky evening light. His new bride was sitting among her sisters, who were fussing around her and still chattering excitedly. By the light of the fire, he took in her simple beauty, her glowing skin and the tilt of her chin. His eyes traced her delicate collarbone and the slender fingers she touched it with. He wanted to touch her skin, too. He wanted to draw his fingers along the fine down that glistened on her arms in the firelight.

The wine had relaxed him, disinhibited his thoughts, and he remembered the preoccupation, the distraction she had been for so long. He remembered how he would return alone after mealtimes to his mattress on the floor of the fleece shed, distracted by her. He remembered his arousal at the thought of her form, and how he would relieve the tension of his sexual urges. And he would ponder the power the girl had over him to cause such a powerful and irrepressible urge. Part of him had wanted to reject her from his thoughts for the effect she had on him, for the aching she caused in his body. And another part was in wonderment and lust at her bodily charms. And now, she was his wife.

Asaph led her away from the celebrations and across the dusty track to the rooms they would now call home. The crackling fire, the music and the drunken merriment faded as they left the revelling behind. Asaph opened the door. His wife smiled up at him. Her eyes were soft and relaxed and her heart full of the merriment. Asaph was now looking at her in a different way. The wine he had consumed and the memories of his lustful nights brought the anticipation of the consummation of their marriage into sharp focus.

She averted her eyes. Their usual dreamy openness was deflected and hidden in her downturned gaze. She had been told by her mother of a girl's wedding night, of what to expect. Other women gossiped and exchanged stories, speaking about their obligations, their duty, their pain. She was suddenly feeling anxious and alone. She was away from the family that had always been an extension of her. And now she was a woman in her own right. A wife. It was new, it was frightening, and she stood motionless in the doorway.

Asaph sensed her fear. The men had told him their stories, too. A husband's rights now they were wed. She was now his property, his wife. It must be done, it was expected; he must make this woman his own with his body. He must consummate the marriage and claim her with his body. He thought of his lonely nights and the imaginings of her physical form. Her breasts, her thighs. Now it was allowed, it was expected, and the prospect intoxicated him and grew like a spectre in his mind and body. He must prove himself a man. He must take her. He wanted to take her.

He asked her to light the lamps and she moved forward and obediently lit the wicks. The oil burned clear and golden. The flames danced and quivered and sent shadows across the walls. She kept her back to her new husband. The lamps spread a golden rippling glow across the room. Asaph watched the sway of her hips as she moved. His arousal was immediate and strong. He watched her from behind, entranced and lost in her form, his eyes wide and focused on her body. He could take her; he had permission from society, from the world of men; he could do whatever he wanted. It was his prerogative; the men had told him. It was the way of things. An animal urge threatened to overtake him. An urge to overpower her, to prove that she was his. Her shape was illuminated by the lamps. Her hair flowed down over her shoulders; her waist and hips made soft undulating curves, magnetising him to the secret contours and folds of her body beneath her clothes.

He took a step forward. A tunnel vision descended; his unflinching focus was his urge to unite, to penetrate, to take what he wanted, to take what was his. He could think of nothing else. His breathing quickened and his focus sharpened. His lust was the fire behind the focus, the fuel, a fireball burning in his loins and she was his target. His eyes didn't leave the rounded shape of her buttocks. This softness, this firmness, this womanliness – he wanted her body.

His new wife could feel his presence behind her. She could feel his eyes appraising her body like a predator. Like in the stories the women had told her of a man's needs. The back of her neck tensed against his presence. She closed her eyes and found herself mouthing a prayer – to her mother, to someone, to God – to give her strength. And she turned to face Asaph.

Her face was tight, her lips pursed and tears brimmed in her eyes. Asaph looked at her frightened face and she was no longer the faceless body she was a moment before. Something in him broke, his focus cracked and his white tunnel collapsed at the sight of her distress.

He had never seen her frightened. He had never seen fear in her eyes. His heart lurched. It was him that terrified her. His lust, his predatory sexual impulse fell away as he looked into her beautiful eyes, shining with tears of terror. His heart burst with such care and affection for her. The reverence and appreciation and the desire to impress her, to please her, the feelings that underpinned his attraction to her, flooded back through him. Asaph was full of shame. A moment before he had wanted to dominate her, help himself to her body, and now he could not look her in the eyes. He was confused, derailed. He didn't know what to do, or how to be. How could a man reconcile such powerful and contradictory feelings? He didn't know how to be a man. Was he a man or was he a child, or was he both?

He had frightened her and now all he wanted to do was protect her. How had that happened? How could he take what was his, satisfy his needs, consummate the union but protect her from it at the same time? How could that be done?

She looked into her husband's eyes. The threat of the predator was gone and her Asaph was back. She saw his vulnerability. She saw his confusion and shame. They held on to each other's eyes as they found themselves and each other again. They found what connected them, their mutual care. It hung precariously between them; the balance restored. A tender, delicate and fragile balance.

The lamp light flickered, casting their shadows on the walls. Without taking her eyes from his, she lifted her clothes over her head and stood naked before him. He held her gaze. She felt safe while she was held in his eyes, while their deeper knowing was activated and its wisdom guided them both in their fear. Tears brimmed in Asaph's eyes at her beauty, at her mercy, at her trust and her courage. All this he read in her eyes and his own overflowed with tears. Without taking his eyes from hers, he allowed the tears to roll gently down his face. He was matching her bravery, acknowledging it, and he loved her in that moment.

Their eyes still locked, she lifted his clothes above his head, and as she did his chest expanded, his heart grew and he felt like a phoenix arisen. Somehow, she had elevated him, restored him. He stood naked before her and wanted to encircle her with his field of strength. Not to overpower her but to protect her. He wanted to give her everything now and take nothing.

Moments before, he had felt like a vulnerable child, but with her acceptance of his fear, he now felt like a king. Her eyes softened and, without moving, her body seemed to yield in response to his nobility. They did not touch each other. Their eyes stayed locked and she surrendered into his safety, and she melted and merged with the energy of her king.

Their bodies responded with an intelligence of their own, born from the knowing in their eyes and the energetic charge between them. She became like an expanded electromagnetic field and he became like a focused current of electricity. And the current entered the field and they cried and they smiled as they surrendered and swam in the currents, the ebb and flow of their bodies, until daybreak.

43

A saph looked across the desert to the horizon. Something was in the air. The land whispered to him and warned him, foretold him of something approaching from afar. He strode slowly back to his home, deep in thought. He was thirty now and older and wiser. With his friend, he had taken over the running of the business. Their brotherly bond had deepened over the years and they knew each was an indispensable part of the success of their lives.

The father was older now and liked to think he was still in charge. Asaph and his friend kindly indulged his occasional directives and interference and then carried on in their own way. All three understood how this worked and the business thrived. They now spun the wool into yarn on a large scale and the younger sisters wove it into fabrics, chattering as ever, and the extending family was provided for by the profits of the business.

His friend grew plumper and had acquired a wife. She indulged his epicurean passions and fed him generously, and in many ways, she stoked his buoyancy and joy of life.

Asaph's wife had born him four healthy children. He felt proud and protective of his family. He was strict and fair as they explored the boundaries of behaviour, but he was never driven to strike them. His wife's serenity abided and her stillness, her ocean, anchored him in their life together.

It was a hot day and the children had sought the cool and shade inside. Asaph paced restlessly around the wool-processing buildings. In the intervening years, they had grown in size, another block had been built and he had added another room to his dwelling. This was his whole world.

The sun was beating down. Its intensity had a message. Asaph found it hard to receive. Its flavour was unpalatable. He had learned to listen to nature. It had guided him and provided an unerring wisdom, some wordless direction should he chose to pay attention to it. Following these intuitions had always served him well.

Asaph called a meeting with his friend. For all that he was full of ebullience, he was also shrewd and discerning, and he had learned to trust his friend's judgement and intuition. His friend, too, had felt the unease. They had heard word from the itinerant shepherds that trouble was brewing beyond the horizon. Some people had begun to leave, seeking refuge in their village and towns beyond. They came carrying their possessions and they looked strained and exhausted. There were tails of skirmishes. The Romans were tightening their authority over their lands. They had squeezed out some fringes of society and brought in pernicious laws to limit their activities. Their centuries-old traditions and their lineage of landholding was being threatened. Things had escalated and soldiers now enforced the governance of the towns with increasing zeal, quashing any resistance with violence. The stories were disturbing. The shepherds were moving to different areas; they were no longer free to roam around with liberty to find the best grazing. Indeed, supplies of wool this spring were much reduced and the prices had risen. The two men shared their concerns. Not just for the business, but for the uncertainty and disturbance that was close by.

Outside again, Asaph let the sun burn its message down on his back and he knew things were about to change for him, and not for the better. Asaph was silent over the mealtime that evening. He sat now at the head of his own table and his heart felt heavy. He did not want to worry his wife. He didn't want to drop a stone into her still inner pond. He wanted to preserve her depths. He wanted to protect the magical black stillness of her womanliness, through which, in their union, he entered what felt like the deep mysteries of Mother Earth herself. This preciousness was under threat and he wanted to guard it.

Scouts from the Roman army walked into the village along the same dusty road Asaph had walked all those years before. Their property on the outskirts was one of the first the soldiers came across. The soldiers arrived in pairs and seemed to spread through the village like an infestation of unwelcome insects. He saw them as a party of cockroaches, leaving no crevice unexplored or uninvaded as they crawled around in their brown, leathery casings, spreading filth. And in his mind's eye, he saw a pool of blood seeping across the ground.

Asaph and his friend were in the fleece shed when two soldiers walked in. They made their announcement. A directive from highest governance. They delivered their order like hard, implacable automatons. Even the stench of the fleeces didn't seem to penetrate their uncompromising facades.

They must leave their homes, their business, and must join the Roman army in allegiance to their leader. The Roman army was extending its territory, taking ground, and they would be conscripted into the army or their fleeces would burn and the safety of their families could not be guaranteed.

The soldiers read from a scroll, a rolled vellum parchment with all the gravitas of a binding order. The soldiers walked around the building. There were no other young men. The sisters worked the washing troughs, with Asaph's modified machinery making it lighter work, and they spun and wove.

Asaph felt sick. He felt cornered and powerless and wanted

to lash out at the soldiers who felt entitled to search his property. But with the soldiers carrying lances, with their icy resolve and army of fellow cockroaches throughout the village, he thought better of it. Their details were taken and they were told to leave at first light and report to the fort in the town across the horizon.

Asaph thought of his wife and children, and he knew that if it would protect them and the sisters, then he would go. He reasoned that maybe it would not be for a long time and he could return and continue his life. Some wiser part of him doubted that it would be that simple. Asaph started planning. His father-in-law was no use to the Romans; he was too old, but he would be able to oversee the business. The women were skilled, but they would be vulnerable. He knew those left behind would face difficult and straitened times.

The soldiers left. There was nothing in their manner that allowed any room for negotiation. It was clear they would use the necessary force to achieve their ends to recruit men for their army. Non-compliance would end in brutality, and he suspected that compliance would also end in brutality. Asaph and his friend looked at each other in silence. At least they would be together. It was clear which of them would fare better in the rigours of life as a soldier. Asaph would look out for his friend.

In the morning, Asaph took the parcel of food his wife pressed into his hand. She gripped her hands over his and over the parcel and held them tight. She could do this for him – parcel up a meal. It was all she could do. They had barely slept. Their minds were racing, and in the darkness, the fear came over them in waves and their bodies responded. Asaph knew they had created another life that night. The current and the field had created in defiance, in desperation. A new life was created from a primal need to hold onto each other, their lives and their liberties in the face of their imminent removal.

44

Asaph and his friend made their way through the town. Neither of them was used to such a dense population and such a tumult of activity. It was hot and it was loud. People were shouting and clamouring to get attention for their wares and services. Asaph had to shout and barge to carve a path through the melee. He was weary from the long walk, short-tempered and in tight-lipped resistance to this situation they had no choice but to accept.

It rankled. Asaph was angry. The theft of his liberties and his subjugation to the control of others ignited the memories of his childhood. He mulled over how his power had been taken away then, his father's forcing him to work for the oil merchant. The violence that was employed. He chewed it over and over and the prospect of servitude again, of giving himself to someone else's cause, burned like acid in his guts.

He didn't allow himself to think of the home he had just left. He blocked it from his mind. Just like when he was a boy and couldn't bear to think of his home and his mother. He would not think of it.

The situation was galling. It burned away at his insides. He could feel acid leaking into him as his body balked. Inwardly, he simmered and stewed in the toxic juices of his resistance to the theft of his personal authority. He could not accept it. He remained tight-lipped and heavy-browed as he pushed a path through the heaving mass of people and animals. He did not want to be here. Every fibre of his body revolted. Every cell burned with injustice.

Asaph ignored his friend, who followed in his wake and had fallen into his own silence. He knew not to speak to Asaph. He knew his mood was explosive and he had no desire to detonate him. So, he walked behind him, nursing his own fears and trepidation. This was indeed a challenge to his resolute upbeat view of life. But even as he steered through the clouds of dust and gagged at the putrid aromas, his eye was drawn to the traders scrapping for a living. There was something in their hustling and their jostling for business that lifted him. This was his excitement, haggling for a good deal, and it was the only thing in this place that felt familiar to him and he clung onto it. He caught snatches of bartering, glimpses of the theatre he knew and loved. This would not be for him now, he suspected, but it momentarily entertained and distracted him.

The walk had exhausted him. He was more given to letting donkeys and mules take the burden of travel. He was working hard to keep up with Asaph, who was fit and lean and whose anger fuelled his unrelenting pace. Here and there, wandering through the crowds, he saw Roman soldiers milling around, letting their presence be known. As he and Asaph moved along, the crowds began to thin, but the soldiers seemed to increase in number.

The fort sprawled before them; the long, high walls were imposing. Still, the friends did not speak. There was nothing to say. Best to keep their feelings inside. The two men paused outside the ominous, towering, gated entrance. The glare and commands of the guarding soldiers meant hesitation was not an option and, with the sun burning on his back like a branding iron, Asaph led them forward.

There were no refinements here. The atmosphere was of all the bawdy and bullying aspects of man Asaph knew well and detested. But to survive, he knew he must find this part in him again. And with his own anger at the situation, it would be easy for him to find. They were barked and shouted at and barged into a kind of holding room with other recruits. Asaph thought of the sheep. Their identical faces and marble eyes, and he had become one of them with his fellow men herded together for a common purpose. Some protested and their angry bleats were curbed with blows to the ribs from the soldiers. Their hair was removed, roughly shorn and deloused. The indignity burned in Asaph.

Heaps of military tunics were piled on the floor. They were filthy and smelled no better than the piles of fleeces. They were clearly the tunics from dead soldiers. Some were blood-stained and all were rank and filthy with sweat and grime. Asaph didn't hesitate with his selection. He took the next one and inwardly gave a nod to the fellow man it had belonged to and didn't dwell on the reason why he no longer needed it.

Asaph looked around. Soldiers were stationed in every corner. Their faces empty; their eyes hard and vacant. They were long stripped of their own freedom, their own free thinking – if they had ever had any. Through a dimly lit vestibule, Asaph could see barrack rooms, each with wooden bunks against the walls. Asaph felt something deep inside being crushed by the uniformity of this place. The stripping of individuality felt dehumanising. He had been free to live by his own conscience and entrepreneurial instincts this last decade or more. He balked. Inside, he was twisting in an unspoken revolt.

Still Asaph had not spoken to his friend. They were assigned to the same bunk. Outwardly, by their lack of engagement, they appeared as strangers and not brothers-in-law and best friends.

Asaph was unreachable. The bitterness at his childhood, his father, the oil merchant and their abuse of him flooded his awareness. He realised that he had put all that behind him and it had become forgotten as he had built his new life. But now there was no escaping the unresolved injustice, the pain of the beatings, the scrabbling to retain his own dignity. His refusal to turn off his inner Light, his resistance to the oppressors – it all came back. It had festered without him realising it. It had been left unattended in the depths of his heart, and with this place, this forced compliance to the will of others, it was sending him again into a white tunnel of rage.

There was to be an address, an announcement. The recruits were herded outside into a courtyard. Shorn and tunicked, they were a shabby and disparate collection of disoriented men. They stood close together. The sun baked down. Asaph didn't acknowledge any of his fellow recruits. He was isolated and deeply troubled by his own inner turmoil.

A uniformed soldier stepped forward and demanded their attention. He shouted an introduction of their great military commander. They would pledge their allegiance to him. They were commanded to recognise him with a salute, to revere their esteemed leader. The forced subjugation of his own power in deference to another was like a fire blazing at the edges of Asaph's cauldron of rage.

A man strode into the arena. He had seen more decades of life than Asaph, but his thighs and calves were still thick and muscular, and he moved stiffly with his powerful bulk. He was broad and thickset, with a solid, sinewy neck and a wide face set with a sneer and the jutting chin of a tyrant. This man had spent many years honing his power in the Roman elite. His air was of ruthless control, and Asaph sensed that this man would be quick and merciless in brandishing his power to maintain it.

Asaph was close enough to see that he was sweating profusely, his bulk compressed in his heavy uniform. His brow was wide and square, sun-baked like leather and creased with deep lines. Beneath his left eye, a jagged and discoloured scar sliced down the side of his face. It was old and deep. Beads of sweat tracked down its bumpy line of peaks and gunnels. Asaph already detested this brute before he had even spoken a word.

The commander began his oration by pacing back and forth, making a series of grunts and snorts like a bull. His uniform was embellished. A cape hung from his shoulder and golden adornments flashed in the sunlight, decorating his huge chest. He swung a bludgeon. His beady eyes surveyed the recruits, his lip curled, and eventually his address began.

He laid before them the military campaigns he had masterminded, his victories and the crushing of his opponents. Asaph only heard snatches of his bragging. He couldn't bear to listen. His military esteem, the gratitude of the emperor, his decorations, a frenzy of self-inflation. It was clear he believed his own supremacy and that made him deadly. The commander forged on. His voice shook and he began weeping at his own deluded brilliance. It had been with his influence that Yeshua, the one they called the son of God, had been executed, crucified, annihilated. He steadied himself and leaned on his bludgeon as he reeled at his own inflated importance.

Asaph was struck deeply by the name of Yeshua. Time seemed to stand still and the name chimed through deeper and deeper layers of him. He was taken back to that day, when, as a boy, he had stood and watched Yeshua hanging on the cross. His heart was suddenly pained. How had he forgotten those events? He remembered the day the woman Mariam had come to the oil merchant and he had given her his special oil. He remembered her care, her gaze and the rays of light around her. He pictured her ministry at the foot of the cross and her devotion to Yeshua. How she had held her palms up to him with an invocation. How, as a boy, he had watched her and his heart had activated. It had held something – something to do with the woman's actions.

How some trusting and intuitive inner part of him had become a cage, protecting and holding. How he had held and held and held until he thought his body would cleave. It just happened, he just did it, he would not fail her. And he remembered how when it was over, he felt that Yeshua himself had reached down and anointed him with a golden kiss on his head.

The memory of that kiss suddenly evoked a knowing of a divine love. He knew the capacity of a man for unconditional love of all mankind. He understood Yeshua's message that the Kingdom of God was in all men. It washed through him, flooded him with golden Light and he suppressed the rising tears as his hardened heart crumbled. He felt seen; he was not alone. It was as if he had been reminded of his own higher nature in this horrific spectre, as he stood before this self-obsessed, self-aggrandising, grabbing, depraved version of a man.

Asaph tried to cling to this feeling, cling to this salvation, this truth, this life raft, this light in the darkness. But it faded and his present moment began to seep back into his awareness. But he knew what he had felt in his private reverie, his escape from his current suffering, had been real and its memory would sustain him and give him hope.

The dictator was still pacing on his podium and extolling his supremacy. He told them of their privilege to serve him, of his absolute authority over them and their absolute subordination. He roused the gullible men with his bravado and, like panting dogs, they lapped up his bloodthirsty rhetoric. Large factions in the group were bristling. They had found their spokesman, their hero, and they were happy to cling to the hem of his cloak of false power, to align with his righteous superiority and swear their allegiance and carry out his bidding.

Asaph watched the man. He regarded him now with curiosity. He was completely blind to his own ignorance. How did a man become so corrupted and stray so far from the goodness in his heart? So far from the Kingdom of God? How did such darkness and violence proliferate?

This quest for power over others seemed ingrained in the commander; his body was rigid with it, with every cell functioning from a need to win. He was in a permanent white tunnel of focused hatred on an enemy. And unlike his own tunnel vision, which could be broken open with the activation of his conscience, a stepping in of a wiser, more loving aspect, this man's white tunnel was terrifyingly permanent, ingrained over decades, reinforced and strengthened with his continued indulgence and embodiment of it. He had no conscience to appeal to.

Inwardly, Asaph sighed. Some clarity had been restored and he glanced sideways at his friend, who stood next to him. Their eyes met momentarily. His own deflation, trepidation and resignation was reflected in his friend's eyes. They had each other. Their brotherly bond was sealed in that glance. They were not alone and, somehow, they would survive this together.

45

Asaph lay in his bunk. He looked at his hands. They were familiar, like old friends. He had watched them building things, using tools, creating. He had watched them caressing his wife's beautiful skin, his hands calloused and rough. They could never be scrubbed clean. They would never be as clean and soft as his wife's belly. He allowed himself to think of her skin, so often the backdrop to his hands.

He thought how his hands were his loyal and reliable tools. They were capable and clever and they enabled him to bring his ideas into life. They made things, they cherished things, they connected him to things. They were a link, a first point of contact with things outside of himself. When he reached, they would touch. They would let him know the feeling of things; the smooth cheeks of his children, the electricity that ran through them when he touched his wife's body.

He turned them over and examined his palms, their patterns of lines and creases – a unique and familiar map carved into them. He hadn't ever taken the time to think about them, to appreciate them. He was them; they were him; they were how he expressed who he was. They created life for him.

He wondered at the cleverness of his body, how it all worked. How his hands knew his ideas and magically obeyed and carried out his plans, his inventions, his innovations. Ideas came into his head and out through his hands. He reflected on his situation now. He was using his hands to practice pushing spears into imagined enemies, stabbing with daggers, using his hands for killing. And his hands still obeyed and did his bidding, but his heart protested. It screamed out in alarm at the actions of his mind and hands. He had no choice but to ignore the pleas of his heart to survive this situation.

He thought how his heart and mind and hands had worked in perfect harmony in the past decade. How he had been in a flow and how it had served him and all those around him. Without his heart, the system was out of balance and he felt bleak. A reduced man. A heart must be involved in the decision-making. He was convinced of that. He sighed.

The next day, he was marching in a heavy uniform, helmet, weapons and armour. The sun was high in a cloudless sky. The recruits walked for hours in formation, in step, over challenging terrain. Asaph was one of the stronger men. He knew he was being watched, but he hung back and walked beside his friend, who was struggling and falling behind. His friend had lost his lustre since their arrival. He was quiet and something in him seemed broken. He ate meals with no enthusiasm and struggled with the physical demands and rigours of a soldier's training.

Asaph marched beside him. His friend wasn't the only man struggling; many men were tiring, but Asaph could sense his friend's heaviness. He could no longer keep to a straight line. As he weaved, Asaph spoke to him urgently in hushed tones, calling his name, calling him back. He breathed words of encouragement, trying to keep him going, letting him know he was with him and that they could do this. His efforts felt in vain as his friend stumbled. Without a thought, Asaph put his arm around him and kept him on his feet. He urged him to keep going. They were nearly at a rest station. Asaph used all his emotional and physical strength to uplift and will his friend forward.

The Roman commander was sitting on a carriage up ahead, watching his troops as they approached the rest station. He was assessing the fittest, mentally selecting the best, assessing the loyal, sniffing out the men who shared his killer instinct.

He watched Asaph and his struggling friend and a seething mist descended upon him. Which was worse? The pathetic, stumbling soldier or the pathetic man helping him like a baby. What kind of soldier takes his eye off the task and panders to the weakness of others? It revolted him.

He could see the stronger man now talking to the weakling, talking into his ear with his arm around his back, half carrying him against his own body. The Roman commander could not bear the weakness in either of them. The physical feebleness or the soft-hearted feebleness. He let them walk by. Asaph felt the commander's eyes on him. His friend was barely aware of anything as his head lolled forwards and his feet dragged along the ground.

At the rest station, the men stopped to take on water and recover before the march continued. Men broke into groups and sat on the ground. There was banter between the fitter men, those that rose to the challenge. Water and bread were passed between them. Asaph was helping his friend, propping him up and holding water to his mouth, splashing and wiping his face to revive him. His friend was burning up, feverish, and he couldn't eat. Asaph squeezed his hand and his friend looked weakly back at him.

Something in their camaraderie stuck in the commander's throat. He watched them together. It was clear they knew each other well. Their bond was more than that of new acquaintances. It was a weak link in his troops and he eyed them with contempt. Brothers perhaps, he mused. It was an ugly display of weakness and the commander could not bear it. It was unacceptable, intolerable and it would be extinguished. He would make an example of them. He would show the new recruits that this was an unacceptable violation of his code and they would be punished.

The commander groaned as he heaved his bulk to his feet. He leaned on his bludgeon and began pacing up and down in front of the group. Each soldier fell into silence. The commander paced and he knew that, without a word, he had the full attention of them all. His disdain and revulsion at the two men simmered. He watched one caring for the other and it rankled. Was it a wave of perverted jealousy that made him want to eliminate this man's show of affection? His eyes took on a steely focus and his mind wormed and writhed through his options to punish the straggling weakling and the pitiful excuse of a man who was babying him.

He moved towards the two men. The other soldiers were silent, tense, fixed on the impending drama, knowing these men were in deep trouble. Asaph sat on the ground with his friend, who was exhausted and sodden with sweat. His friend managed a faint smile of resignation at the hopelessness of the situation. They both knew he would not be able to carry on.

The Roman commander knelt down, close to Asaph's shoulder. Everything was silent. His friend's eyes widened and Asaph froze, feeling the sudden hostile presence bearing down on him. The commander leaned in from behind Asaph until his face was beside his ear. Asaph could smell his stale breath and sweat. He felt the lust for blood in his heavy, menacing breathing.

The commander relished this moment, when his prey had frozen. He lingered and extended this moment for his own delight, inwardly purring with an exquisite satisfaction. "I have no room for weaklings, for feeble little girls, in my army." He was beside Asaph's ear and speaking into it, but looking ahead into his friend's face. He let the words and their implications hang in the air. It was delicious. He pressed the tip of his tongue against the roof of his mouth and held his breath, and let the sublime current of power and dominance permeate his entire body. They were at his mercy. And he had none.

The sweat was beading on his face and he took a heavy breath. His lips quivered with excitement. He spoke in Asaph's ear. "Finish him off. Put the runt out of his misery."

The instruction took a moment for Asaph to process, but as the commander pressed in closer, his ox's head millimetres from his own, he knew he was being ordered to kill his friend. Asaph felt sick.

"You are a man, are you not?" he hissed in Asaph's ear. "Then prove it. Finish off this worthless piece of shit." He paused for effect and softened his tone. "Or are you not man enough?" He began to speak slowly and precisely for avoidance of doubt. "Take your dagger and push it into this heap of shit. Finish him. Do it *now*."

Inside, the commander was inflating as the delicious cocktail of power and control electrified and scintillated his senses. He looked side-on into Asaph's face, curled a quivering lip and raised an eyebrow. Asaph felt a hard steel blade upon his neck, pressing flat against his skin. The Roman commander held the probing point with just enough restraint to not pierce the skin.

Asaph looked at his friend, his dearest friend, like a brother to him. Inside his mouth, he bit his lip and suppressed his emotions as he looked into his eyes. He must kill his friend or be killed himself. Wide-eyed, they stared at each other and tried to convey their feelings, their loyalty, their trusted bond. It was beyond impossible what Asaph was being commanded to do. His friend's eyes were full of fear and they spoke silently to each other. They understood each other. The friend's face began to soften with his love for this man, his beloved friend, with a knife pressed to his neck.

Asaph, this good man, had always been his greatest ally and supporter and, in that moment, he realised that Asaph had always been his hero, his inspiration, and he tried to convey this to him. He was not as worthy as Asaph; he knew he was a lesser man and it was right. If one of them was to die, it should be him and he accepted his fate. He wanted Asaph to know it was okay, that he understood, that he did not blame him. He wanted him to do it now, finish him off. He couldn't bear to watch Asaph's torture. Take me, he begged with his eyes. Take me and save yourself. His friend was willing him to do it. Do it quickly; take me and save yourself.

The knife point pricked at Asaph's neck. The commander smirked. Asaph moved his hand to feel for his dagger, which hung in his belt. His hand, his hand that extended out from his heart, which created and made the world better. His fingers touched the top of his dagger. But his hand would not obey. His hand seemed to refuse the command of his mind and instead obeyed the voice of his heart.

He looked at his friend and his love for him was suddenly overpowering. Asaph's heart burst with a love for him and a love for all mankind. A golden burst of Light blinded him and he surrendered into its arms as the commander's blade pierced his skin and slowly plunged into his neck. Asaph fell from his knees to the floor and the commander followed, leaning over him, driving the dagger in up to its hilt.

Asaph was pulled from his body by the golden Light. From above, he watched his mortal form. A pool of scarlet blood spread across the ground like a red velvet cloak around his slumped body. The last beats of his mortal heart pumped, and the velvet cloak grew and spread. Asaph was free.

46

The Commander's knife squelched as he pulled it from Asaph's flesh and he slowly wiped it on his tunic. He felt calm; he felt at peace. All was well inside of him. A kind of relief prevailed from his satiation; the calm after his own storm. He levered his bulk off the ground and leaned heavily on his bludgeon. He replaced his dagger and, without a glance at Asaph's friend, he walked away.

The soldiers' eyes followed the commander. Some had found a strange and macabre thrill at what they had witnessed; some had been horrified; and all of them were now vigilant and on high alert. Asaph's blood seeped from the dagger across the commander's tunic, a warm and sticky stain of his butchery.

He ordered the soldiers to fall back into line and swiftly they obeyed. The troops marched forward. A little more orderly, a little more slickly, a little more alert and with two less to their number. Without looking back, the commander's carriage rattled alongside his troops, who, as intended, were sharper, more attentive and obedient.

The sound of the soldiers leaving faded into the distance. The friend was left for dead. Asaph's lifeless body lay slumped in front of him. He was transfixed by the grisly sight before him and he could not move. He watched Asaph's red velvet cloak crawl across the ground towards him. It was as if it was reaching for him, the last part of his bonded brother, alive and coming towards him, reaching for him. It was moving, thick and lustrous, and it felt the only part of him that was still alive.

A bird fluttered down and pecked at the scattered remnants of bread. A stout white bird. It hopped around next to the men. It stayed for several moments, not frightened by them. Was it looking at him? It seemed that way. Something in its simplicity, its innocence, its lightness made everything seem simple and uncomplicated.

The cloak had reached its fullest as the last of Asaph's vital fluid drained from his wound. The friend sank his palm into the pool of blood. With his other hand, he took his own dagger from his side and felt nothing as he sliced deeply across his own wrist. He felt no pain as he watched great pulses of his own blood pump into the scarlet cloak. It felt simple, right, honourable, the only option. He watched their blood unite and merge together. A rightness, a parity, an honouring.

He dropped his dagger and leaned forward and kissed Asaph's head. Tears came and, as he weakened, he lay down beside him with his arm around him. He felt light; they were together. He faded from consciousness until all became white and clear and peaceful. His light body was lifted up and he rested in the feathers of the angels around him.

Below, in the heat of the sun, their blood slowly congealed. It was baked dry and their blood bond was cemented.

47

Everyone was horrified and torn to shreds by the loss of their two beloved men. The women's hearts were broken and the old father was felled, torn down, shattered. A light in the family was extinguished.

It was as if a heavy blanket of despair, misery and hopelessness was cast over all of their lives. Their grief ran deep; it was profound and debilitating. They did the best they could with the business, but it was a joyless necessity. They tried to steer an empty, rudderless ship without their son and brother, and without Asaph, and they eked what living they could from the wreckage. Things fell into disrepair and there was no one to patch things together. The father tried his best, but he was utterly broken by the loss of his son. Each effort to sustain the business was a wrenching reminder of what he had lost.

At first, the father wept openly; he was inconsolable. He rejected his daughters' attempts at comfort and sought solitude spending many hours withdrawn from them all, alone and consumed by his grief.

Some deep and essential part of him had fractured, leaving a gaping wound so wide it might never scab over. It was an open wound. Its nerve endings were frayed and exposed and painfully activated by constant memories of his son. He was so proud of him, his only son; he was everything. He saw himself in the maleness he had passed on to him. He saw his male influence reflected back to him. He remembered his son as a boy. His great joy at having produced a son, a continuation of himself, a successor, a son to take over the business and continue the family line.

He hadn't realised how much he had invested in his son, what expectations he had had. He assumed that, in time, he would have sons himself, that the male bloodline would continue and proliferate. He felt it had been his duty to produce a son, a bloodline, an heir, a future.

And his hopes and expectations were hanging in shards around him. Sharp stabbing fragments of what might have been. They punctured his heart and his mind tormented him with unbidden memories and images of his son. The stories of injustice that ran rampant through his mind plagued him in the day and robbed him of sleep at night. And he missed his son's simple good cheer and ebullience, his joking and teasing, his gentle chiding of him. Their talks of an evening long into the darkness. He just missed him and his heart cleaved.

It was a deep river of pain, of slow unfathomable depths. Deep and powerful primal currents buffeted the riverbed of his soul. Currents of unbearable pain surged and threatened to surface and he braced himself against them. He closed his eyes and turned his head in some reflex, a visceral attempt to escape its rising. He squeezed his eyes tight to stem the waters from breaking the dam and squeezing through him as tears. He braced his heart against the pain and the wave subsided, absorbed back into the depths, where it would lurk in the blackness – only to build up into another tidal wave, and in some unexpected moment it would erupt on the surface and crash through him in a tsunami of grief he was helpless to contain. He feared he would be swept away by it; he wanted to be swept away by it, submerged, taken, drowned.

But his breath would come back to him and his eyes would open and he would stand stripped and alone in the desolation, the bleak and empty wasteland, the barren desert of his life without his son.

He had failed as a man. He had failed to protect his son and failed to provide men for the family, for their future. He had imagined that he would age with his son and his crop of healthy grandsons as a proud man. He would sit under the canopy after evening mealtimes, reclining, with his hands resting on his belly, smiling and seeing the future he had made blossoming and burgeoning around him. He would fade away, having done his duty. But there was no son and there had been no grandsons; there was no future.

It had been a mystery why his son's wife had born him no live children. It hadn't worried him; he had always had faith that his son would one day produce sons of his own. But now his bitterness turned to that barren wife and another wave built inside him.

He had other grandsons – his daughters were prolific in their child bearing – but they were other men's babies, from the lines of other fathers. His own masculine line was finished. The blood from father to son to son was finished, brutally terminated. It was over, his life felt over.

Over time, with the father's repeated efforts to suppress the waves, the gaping wound knitted together and scabbed over. The scab was rigid, with hardened inflexible edges, a piece of gristle that sealed his heart, protecting it from the pain but also preventing it from flexing and flowing and feeling the joy of life.

The business floundered and his health declined. The daughters had husbands, but no one took on the business. It became a monument, a mausoleum, a crumbling reminder of his son. Everyone knew not to speak of him, not to poke a stick into the beehive of the father's pain. They obeyed his unspoken will to consign the business to the past – to let it and their fortunes wither, along with the memory of their brother.

As the months passed, no one spoke of the death. The silence reinforced the scar tissue and pushed the wound deeper. And by the father not speaking of him, and forbidding the family to do so, their own grief was unexpressed and their happy memories stultified. The family's psyche took on the unexpressed pain of the father's devastating loss. It reverberated in the family. It was held inside them all and the unfinished, unhealed heartbreak continued in the collective wound of the generations who followed. It whispered through them and it limited them like a hovering shadow.

48

A brisk breeze lifted the sand and carried it through the air. It was cool; it was the end of the day. Asaph's wife was exhausted. The baby was heavy in her body. Every breath and every heartbeat were for the two of them. Her time was near. She was profoundly sad and prone to tears at her circumstances. She had lost her husband, her beloved. They had understood one another. It had been a deep union, of their bodies and the highest aspects of their natures. They had a reverence for each other, an appreciation and an allowing of all parts of the other. They knew each other's vulnerabilities and didn't use them to reduce the other, to reduce their union. They made space for them and somehow it elevated and deepened their devotion.

And now she was without him and her life felt diminished. She needed him to instruct and discipline the children, and to provide for them. She missed his dependability, resourcefulness and protection. And she missed his face, his body, the beingness of him. She could still picture his face, but it was getting harder to recall and it panicked her that it would fade forever. She looked for him in the faces of her children and saw his features smiling back. She saw his hair and his eyes. And she saw his mannerisms. How was it that an expression, a way of standing, the tilt of a head, something so non-physical could be seen in them? She watched her eldest son as his jaw moved and lodged to one side when he was concentrating, just as his father's had. Had he copied that from his father? She didn't think so; he didn't even realise he was doing it.

Asaph's mannerisms expressed in their children brought joy and pain in equal measure. Her heart was still heavy and she longed for her husband. Sometimes, in clearer moments, she found comfort in an acceptance, a trust in something greater. A trust that whatever the essence of him was, that essential non-physical part, that part she saw in his eyes on their wedding night, that it was real and it could never really die and be extinguished.

She thought of that essence of Asaph as she combed her daughter's hair. She made methodical, slow, rhythmical strokes and that part of him that seemed lost, out in the unknown mystery of it all, seemed to crystallise and take form and she would feel him near to her. He leaned in and she could feel his cheek on hers and the tears rolled down her face. And she would try to hold onto it – she wanted to hold onto Asaph – but he would vanish and she was left sad and wistful. She wiped the tears away and forced a smile as her daughter turned and ran off at the first chance to escape the comb.

The children were already forgetting their father. In the months since his death, he had faded for them and the younger children would not remember him. Their lives were full, there were many cousins and she was glad they were not suffering as she was. She tried not to dwell on it all. She had to get on with her lot. Her days were busy; the family helped her and she was glad of them. The sisters who had fussed around her excitedly in the joy of her wedding day fussed around her again, but this time with solemnity and care and support. She ate with them now and as the baby grew, they took on more of her chores and looked after the children.

At night, she lay alone in the bed she had shared with Asaph. She had become more accustomed to his physical absence. The children sometimes crawled in beside her and their small warm bodies comforted her in the long, dark nights when sleep evaded her. It was these times that her loss revisited her and its magnitude felt at its greatest. These were the times when her faith faltered and her grip on the hope that things would get better would slip through her fingers, until she hung by a thread above a looming chasm in the lonely and never-ending bleak hours before sunrise.

In these hours, the only other wakefulness was in the baby inside her. As everyone slept, the baby kept her company in the insomniac's vigil for the dawn. She placed her hands on her belly. Her insides were compressed, her lungs squashed. Her fingers ran over it, taut and rippled with the red lines of skin stretched to its limit. She watched the baby roll, dragging its elbow along the underside of her belly in a subterranean arc, before disappearing again beneath the surface.

Asaph's baby. The baby that would never know its father; the baby that was conceived in some primitive instinct to seal their union, to stamp and declare a future together for themselves in the uncertainty that prevailed. Something to ensure Asaph would come back.

Her sisters tended to her. The labour pains were strong. Part of her was frightened to bring this fatherless child into the world. Each day of its life, another day further from the memory of him. Her body heaved and she roared with the pain. She roared with the pain of her opening body and she roared with the anger of her grief, the anger at her future and she roared at God.

As the waves of pain took her over, she surrendered into the power of her body. She let the power surge through her like a volcano, erupting in her womb and a flamethrower blistering through her heart. Her awareness expanded and she transcended and joined a primordial space, a primal knowing of Mother, of the Great Mother, the Goddess Mother Earth. She became an animal; she let go into the fiery pain and her body opened and the volcano pushed the child through its mouth, through its ring of fire, into the hands of her sister and the arms of Mother Earth. Its slippery, writhing body joined the realms of the mortal, joined the consciousness of Mother Earth. The baby gasped its first breath of its incarnation and became its own life.

Asaph's wife collapsed back with exhaustion, relief and exhilaration, and she reached for her child. It was a baby boy. His barrel chest and round belly heaving like bellows as his new lungs filled and emptied. She held his body close to her. Her shaking hands traced the wet and bloodied fronds of his hair and she sobbed at the beautiful gift she had been given. And she sobbed for Asaph, for the beautiful gift that had been taken away.

Some days later, Asaph came to her in the night. He desperately wanted her to know that he was there. He pushed into her awareness with his love for her and he leaned into her dreams. His sense of duty was urgent; his need to take care of what was his responsibility. He wanted to tell her that he was still there, and that he would always be there for her and the child. He needed to know that she understood. She felt him there; she felt his commitment, his devotion and his sense of loyalty.

Asaph pressed in as she connected to him. He would not fail her. As he had once held strong and not failed the woman at the foot of the cross, so he would not fail his wife. He clung to her; he held onto her. Her situation, and his responsibility for it, pained him deeply.

And the angels lifted him away; he could not stay – it was not the way of things. And he took his wound with him. The pain of failing her, of leaving her without him when she had depended on him. The pain of abandoning her and of letting her down burned in him and branded its imprint at his very core.

49

Mother Earth turned, and turned. Many years passed by and many fortunes had changed. The Roman commander was hanged from a tree by his wrists, strung up high like an animal on a butcher's hook. The people passed by; some ignored him, turning their heads away. Some spat at him, mocked and taunted him with insults. Others stood and watched, relishing his suffering. Children looked up, wide-eyed, at the hanging monolith. No one helped him.

As he was left hanging, his panic rose. He appealed to them, he beseeched them, he'd been misunderstood, they'd got it all wrong. But no one would listen; no one could be coerced. The pain burned in his shoulders and he knew his chances of salvation were fading. Self-pity rose up; he was swallowed by an indulgent wave of his own victimhood, and he gasped and sobbed and snivelled and begged for mercy to the passers-by. He grovelled like a wretch and pleaded, but to no avail, and so he thrashed around like a tantrumming child at their rejection. Children played nearby, oblivious to his rancour as he swung like a bulky pendulum. The children ignored him, too; they rolled their dice and they laughed. The sun showed no mercy either. For days, he hanged and baked, rotting in his own acid. His parched tongue was silenced, his shoulders dislocated, and he swung and leaked and desiccated. The final moments of his asphyxiated delusions were flooded with a seething incandescence, a hatred for humanity, an outward-pointing poisoned arrow to all mankind. *I hate you all*! And he was dead.

And the angels descended and took him in their arms. To the angels, he was as innocent as the children playing at his feet.

And his life was shown to him. He looked down on the day he was born. The first child, much wanted and doted upon by his mother. Idolised and indulged by her, she poured her love into him as an antidote to her loveless and violent husband. He had to give up his mother's breast when his younger brother was born. Hovering nearby and filled with jealousy, he watched the baby suckling. "You must be a big boy now," his mother had said. But he didn't want to be a big boy; he wanted his mother's love and undivided attention. He began to hate his baby brother for stealing his mother and he pinched him and twisted his little arms.

It alienated his mother more; she chided him and redoubled her affections for the infant. She gazed into his newborn eyes as she had once done with his own. And as they grew up, his mother favoured the easy, biddable younger son and the difficult, aggressive firstborn was increasingly ostracised. The angels showed him how his insecurity and rejection became bitterness and jealousy, and had turned him into a monster, controlling all those around him to get the devotion and attention he craved. He took what he wanted. He thought his suffering entitled him to it.

As they grew up together, the younger, wiser brother felt compassion for his troubled older sibling. The Roman took advantage of his care, manipulated his higher conscience and misused his wise counsel to further his ambitions.

The angels showed the Roman how his brother, in his simple brown robes, had intercepted the little girl he had raped, as she ran into the desert after Yeshua had been killed. How he had found her in despair and taken her back to the safety of her mother. His brother drew a line; it was too much. He had gone too far and he challenged the actions of his older brother. He withdrew his support. The unrepentant Roman raged at his brother's disloyalty and an uncrossable rift was cleaved between them.

Without his brother's wise counsel, the Roman indulged his excesses, his thirst for power over others, and he wrought havoc and destruction. He became like a deluded maniac, out of control, lost in his deeply embittered rage, and he sought greater and greater atrocities to satiate it. This had been his life.

And his brother now stood beside the tree. He looked up at the swinging carcass of his older brother. The tree creaked as it held its gruesome burden, humbly accepting its obligation to provide the gallows for mankind's unfathomable actions.

It was deserted. Just the tree and the swinging Roman and his brother. The air was still; the innocent leaves whispered on the gallows and the rope creaked. The Roman's lifeless bulk hung like a piece of fetid meat. His parched mouth was open and flies crawled into it and his other orifices, looking for a bed of flesh to lay their eggs on. Carrion birds had pecked at the meat of his face. Peck, peck, peck.

The brother levered his long limbs up to the hangman's branch. His wingspan was as wide as an archangel and, with a knife, he sawed through the rope at his brother's wrists. The fibres sprung free from their tension with each cut. He looked at the clawed-over fingers, bloodied and calloused and responsible for untold evil. They were the first to rot, their blood supply severed by the rope. His murderous hands finally incapacitated, deactivated, severed from the motor of his mind. The rope twanged and thinned until the corpse of his brother fell to the ground in a heavy, thudding lifeless collapse. And there he lay in the dust.

The brother climbed down and stood beside him, deep in thought. His brother's body was there, but where was all the hatred and angry life force? It had coalesced into a coagulation of a lifetime of evil thoughts and brutal actions. And it was out there somewhere. A nebulous mass of darkness with no host anymore. The Roman had created it and it had fed off him and become its own living entity. Without its host, where was it now?

He pondered on how he had been the first. He had been the one who first ignited his brother's insecurities and received the first backlash. He had begun the cycle culminating in his brother's mania and the untold suffering of others. He had never known life without its impact.

The brother felt calm. He pondered the inevitability, the futility, the pointlessness of it all, the predictable outcome. What had been the point of that life? No answers came. He died as he had lived, in a world of inner and outer misery. An insatiable tyrant. And for what? A legacy of suffering and pain proliferating in his victims and their families long after his death, reverberating through generations.

The brother walked away. And as he stepped forward, he felt the shadow of his brother fall from him, the badge of association. It was over. He walked and walked and walked, leaving behind the crumpled cloak of the shadow of his brother. A cloak imbued with shame. The shame of being a man. The shame of what a man was capable of doing; the darkest nature of a man. And he left him to the buzzing flies and the pecking birds and the angels.

Part Three

50

eron's story is one of the suffering of women at the hands of unbalanced patriarchal forces.

Asaph's story is one of the suffering of men at the hands of unbalanced patriarchal forces.

In visions, I found Heron – a representation of the wound of my sacred feminine aspect. As I healed and integrated her in my consciousness, through the Law of Attraction, Asaph and his story came to me – a representation of my sacred masculine aspect. Balance, always balance.

These elements were reunited within me and Heron's muteness was healed, and this story emerged as a modern-day message of the implications of feminine and masculine power imbalance. Of the ramifications for humanity of ignoring the feminine aspect today. It comes now as an invitation to embrace the feminine, the vulnerability, and to give it space to heal. It comes as a shining light for the rising feminine in all of us. And the ultimate sacred feminine, Mother Earth, shares her message of unconditional love:

So tenderly I will say that we all need holding with compassion. We all need holding in the arms of the ultimate Great Mother of us all, held by her unconditional love. It is the thing that is needed now, regardless of gender. We all need holding in love.

Allow yourself to feel your own connection to the bosom of the Great Mother Earth. To be comforted, held, nurtured and restored to balance by her.

That is all; just connect to the heart of Mother Earth for she lives in you. She lives and breathes and feels like all sentient beings. Allow her to heal you with her loving embrace. Imagine it, picture it, feel it and you will know it is real. Mother Earth loves you. She will always love you. Whatever you do to her, she will always love you. She doesn't judge you; she wants to guide you back to yourselves, to your authentic power. She speaks to your golden grain. She reaches up, trying to enrich it, imbue it, expand it and help it blossom.

It saddens her that you cannot see that you are all brothers and sisters, that you are all her children, and she loves you all. It pains her to see you hurting one another in battles, small and large. For you are part of her; you are nature. You are her nature. And she stands by you, loyal and fierce with her care and protection. She steadfastly reaches up to touch the golden grain in your heart. With tendrils, she licks and laps and encourages it into life. The more you acknowledge her, the more she responds. Her love is endless. Her love is free. Her love is freedom.

Listen for the sound of Mother Earth in your heart. Listen for her; she is calling you now. She invites you to listen to the echoes in your depths, her reverberations caressing your inner beauty, your sacred heart. Allow her. Allow her to help you. The Mother Goddess is whispering, like a breeze through your soul, reawakening, enlivening, blowing away the stagnant dust and revealing the gold beneath. She illuminates the Kingdom of God and the

Queendom of Goddess in your heart, seeking to reunite in the overarching Sovereignty of the Divine within. Balance, balance, always balance.

May you reside in wholeness.

Acknowledgments

W e all hold the keys for each other in life. I would like to thank those who helped unlock me. My teachers, formal and informal, guides seen and unseen, and those that come for healing who teach me so much.

Great bows of gratitude to my children, Ruby, Ed and Grace. You are the best and have taught me in a million ways how to find the mother in myself. I love you very much.

I thank the friends and family with whom I am interwoven, for your steadfast support and nourishment in all the ways. My lovely old Dad, Brian, Zoe, Tracey and Jeanette are some very special threads in the tapestry.

With extra special thanks for the joy of Andy, Emma and Liam. Thank you to Andy (again) and Rich for your kingly input and support in bringing my vision to life.

And to Phillipa, a cherished and indispensable queenly thread in the weave, for a lifetime of friendship, laughter, adventure, and without whom this book wouldn't have made it.

And, most importantly, with a grateful heart, I thank my own Mother, who, above all, gave me this precious life.

Final Note

I f you are touched by the themes of this story and would like to stay in touch, you are invited to connect at: www.janicedent. com.

There, you will find a free guided meditation to connect with the heart of Mother Earth: A Walk with Heron.

On the page that follows is the symbol Heron was given at the temple. A symbol of the potential of the human heart to align with and create with the divine. Heaven on Earth. As above, so below.

You are invited to cut it out and, in your own safe and sacred space, to connect with it through the guided meditation. That you may know the healing love of Mother, that your golden grain may illuminate and guide you with its wisdom.

Thank you for reading my book.